Unmasking Aurelio

Published by Azalea Press, LLC

First paperback edition February 2026

Cover design by E.V. Sauvage

Edited by Bonnie Macleod

Chapter art by LadadikArt (Creative Market) and Luisline (Canva Pro)

ISBN 978-1-968219-04-8 (ebook)

ISBN 978-1-968219-05-5 (paperback)

www.stfernandez.com

Dedicated to the Hillcrest Community of San Diego.

Love is love is love is love...

Pronunciation Guide

Akani: Ah-KAH-nee
Atlantis: at-LAN-tis
Bajari: Buh-JAH-ree
Borike'n: Boh-REE-keh-en
Guake'te: gooah-KEH-teh:

Character Pronunciation Guide

Albie: AHL-bee

Atabey: ah-tah-BAY

Aurelio Martenos: Ahoo-REH-lee-oh MAR-teh-nohs

Behuko: beh-HOO-koh

Cathan Rosahan Delmar: KAY-thuhn ROH-sah-hahn del-MAR

Francesca Bonaflyn: Fran-CHEHS-kuh BAH-nuh-flin

Hanna Marrel: HAN-nuh Mar-REL

Jade: JAYD

Phylis: FIL-is

Melysah Velafyn: meh-LIS-uh VEH-luh-fin

Myles Anthysius: Mahyels an-THEE-see-uhs

Neleah Delmar: neh-LEH-uh del-MAR

Roarvyn: ROR-vin

Tyla: TEYE-luh

Vebulah Vella: VEB-yoo-luh VEL-luh
Vick: VIK

Author's Note

Unmasking Aurelio features characters from *The Heir of Atlantis* series. While prior knowledge of the series isn't required, readers should note that this story is far more explicit than my usual work. This is a true Romantasy, with the plot centered on Myles and Aurelio, and it is intended for readers aged 18 and over.

Readers familiar with *The Heir of Atlantis* may find this installment spicier than previous books—Myles and Aurelio were in a mood.

But really, what's wrong with that?

Enjoy!

Chapter One

B REATHS, WARM AND LUSTFUL.

Skin, pebbling.

My cock, stirring in its pocket.

The memory hit me like a wave as I recalled my passion-filled night with my masked lover. His skin was as smooth as the silk I held between my fingers. Sewing to the quiet hum of low house music at the checkout desk of my shop, Enchanted Couture, I could still recall every touch, every submission. There was no failure in remembering how he held me—with a blend of dominance, need, and reverence that had me shifting in my stool.

Goddess, how I wanted another night like that.

But the probability was slim, this I understood. Those were the rules of the Starlit Masquerade. *Come masked. Participate in the sexual revelry. Stay anonymous.* Clean. Simple. No strings attached. Just how I preferred it. However, it didn't mean that the yearning for my masked lover lessened in any way. And yes, in a strange and mysterious way, he felt like mine. After all, he hadn't been with anyone else but me at the masquerade year after year. Well, decade after decade, actually.

We'd been meeting each other annually for the longest time now. And still, I didn't know who he was. Every curve of his body was still etched in my memory, however, from his smooth skin blanketing the defined ridges of his abdomen to the alluring patch of dark hair that led to my happy place. In my mind's eye, his soft lips quirking as he issued a command were clear as day, and the sound of his breath hitching when I obeyed still rang in my ears. His deliciously thick and lovely manhood—

"Ow." A not-so-subtle sting jarred me from the memory, blood welling on the tip of my finger. My scowl met the sewing needle as if it held the sole responsibility for the consequences of my daydreaming. As I grabbed a tissue to stem the bleeding, a couple beyond the storefront window caught my eye, and my gaze snagged on the prominent bondmate marks displayed on the left side of their chests. My mouth instantly twisted into a sneer, and it wasn't due to my pricked finger.

Bondmates.

The Fae the goddess has chosen for you for *all eternity*. A love match designed by destiny. My eyes rolled of their own accord.

What a load of bullshit.

While I couldn't hear their peals of laughter through the storefront window, it still grated on me. How can someone tie themself to one person for the remainder of their Fae days? I hadn't been able to tie anyone down for a third date, let alone an *eternity* together.

Honestly, my dating life had been on the hot mess express for as long as I could remember. I didn't understand the problem. The last time I went on a date, the male in question had cut it short when I ordered my second glass of wine. Granted, it was the most expensive wine on the list, and it had been after I swallowed my last bite of the most lavish steak on the menu, but how else was I supposed to test how far his devotion to me stretched? Better I find these things out immediately than to let the relationship linger.

And how could I ever test if the male possessed the same *je ne sais quoi* that my masked lover had? I'm thoroughly convinced that no one will live up to him and all he has to offer. That's why I've sworn off relationships, especially the ridiculous idea of bondmates.

The bell above the door interrupted my brooding, and I smiled as the courier strolled through the door. "Good day, Phylis."

"Hey there, Aurelio." She pointed at the fabric in my hands. "Working on another ball gown for the masquerade?"

"Of course."

Her shoulders shook as she chuckled with a shake of the head. "It's nine months away."

"One can't be too prepared for the Starlit Masquerade. Besides, how am I supposed to live up to my reputation as the go-to designer for the event? I have to be prepared."

"Well, you know more about these things than I do." She motioned toward her plain Jane, muted-blue uniform. "My fashion sense is lacking."

"You can come by any time after work, and I'd be happy to improve your look." I leaned in conspiratorially. "Free of charge," I offered with a wink.

Phylis rocked on her heels. "I might take you up on that offer. Oh!" She reached into her mail sack and handed me a letter with an official seal stamped in the corner. "For you. It's from the Office of Property Establishment at the palace."

I took it from her with a furrowed brow. "What could this be about?"

"I'm sure it's nothing to worry about. I get loads of those envelopes every day," she reassured me with a quirk of her lips. "Anyway, I'd best be going. The rest of Borike'n will be waiting for their mail, and they get cranky if it isn't on time. Bye, Aury!" With a final wave, she left me and the mysterious envelope alone in my shop.

I wasted no time turning it over and ripping open the flap, and when my eyes scanned the contents of the letter within, my lungs seized.

My building had been sold to Behuko Enterprises.

Excellent.

Just what I needed.

New owner. New problems.

Later that afternoon, I was busy tugging a midnight blue dress onto the mannequin in the storefront window when a tall, lanky figure strolling down the sidewalk came into view, her hips swaying with conviction as those around her held their palms to their hearts in reverence. As awkwardness bloomed on her beautiful features, a grin tugged at my lips.

Tyla had only recently answered the calling of the Bajari—those who were born with one sex but had been called to transform into another. She accepted the blessing during the Bajari Ritual at the Temple of Atabey, where she'd received the invocation from the Priestess to transform. Tyla was still having trouble with Atlantians saluting her with a hand over their hearts as she passed by. Unfortunately, she'd have to get used to it. The Bajari were seen as a good omen and a reminder of the goddess's hope for the future —a sign that her love for her people is infinite.

As Tyla cast a shy yet pleasant smirk at a young man staring at her with hearts in his eyes on the walkway in front of the shop, she opened the door muttering a series of curses under her breath, her long, lethal stilettos clacking on the travertine tiles.

"Greetings, oh hot one."

"Oh, don't you start," she replied, heading immediately for the back of the shop.

"Still having trouble being admired by the masses?"

Tyla paused, her long, pin-straight hair brushing against her lower back as she turned, her rounded human ears cutting through the curtain of hair. "I've had no less than three males beg to present me before the goddess at Guake'te—"

"They do realize you're a human?"

"And two females."

"My, my. That *is* busy."

"So, if you don't mind, I'll be in the back, where I can forget about being offered everlasting love by everyone I pass by."

I glanced over the shoulder of the mannequin with a teasing expression. "However will you pass the time?"

"However I damn well please," she answered as she briskly brushed aside the curtain to the back of the shop.

My lips were held firmly between my teeth to quell the chuckle that threatened to emerge as the skirt of the dress settled on the form. I was smoothing out the fabric when the bell over the door chimed again. Without looking up, I said, "I'm afraid the Bajari is currently occupied at the moment."

"Just as well, because I'm not here for her," a smooth voice replied.

A tremor ran through me.

That voice.

Dear greatest goddess above. That. Voice.

Peeking over the shoulder of the mannequin, I met the beautiful, mahogany-eyed gaze of the male before me.

Myles Anthysius, the queen's Secretary of the Sovereign, was quite possibly the most breathtaking male in all the realm. Not many Water Fae could style their scales like human clothing properly. But Myles Anthysius damn well could. I'd often admired his poise and ability to look dashing in his scales, always styled with a collar that screamed perfection. His dark hair rarely had a strand out of place, and the way his eyes pierced your soul, well... it wasn't a shock that it made my dick twitch. Pulling away my attention, I cleared my throat to dispel my unbound feelings. Emotions like these could be entirely dangerous.

Thou shalt not ogle the Secretary.

Thou shalt think only of the anonymous masked male who is safe.

"Secretary. A pleasure to see you," I greeted.

A kind smile lifted his lips. "I assure you, the pleasure's all mine."

Damn those lips.

Plucking up the courage, I stepped around the mannequin, the velvet fabric of my designer robe brushing against my scaled legs as I reached him. "How can I help you today?" I gave him a once-over, feigning indifference. "Perhaps a new wardrobe to add a little flair to your life?"

"*Yes, Daddy. That's the spot. Harder. Oooooh. Just like that.*"

Pure, utter mortification coursed its way throughout my body and soul as the voice traveled throughout the shop. The accompanying slapping of skin upon skin didn't help either. I tilted my head. "Will you excuse me for a moment?"

"*Fuck, yeah. Right there. Give me that fat fucking cock!*"

"Of course," Myles said with an arched brow.

Scurrying to the back of the shop, I pulled the curtain aside. "Tyla," my voice hissed in a sharp whisper. "What have I told you about watching OnlyFins at the shop?"

She glanced at me with innocence. "I can't help it, Aury. It's Baylah and Rahim. You know they come on randomly. And you know how I feel about scenes involving humans and Water Fae. They're hot to watch."

"Fuck yeah, baby. You feel so good. Getting so wet for Daddy. Come on my cock."

Slap. Slap. Slap.

Tyla did have a point. They *were* hot. But this was the worst timing. "Tyla. Turn. It. Off."

With a sigh, she shut down OnlyFins.

Through the racks of clothing, I hurried to the front of the shop with a straightened spine, trying desperately to act as if the esteemed Secretary hadn't heard that, but when I was met with his knowing expression, I knew I'd massively failed.

"You'll have to forgive her. She's a bad little Bajari. Likes to watch."

Did I just say that?

Judging by the crimson spots climbing up Myles's neck and the subtle twitch of his lips, those words indeed left my mouth.

"Now, how can I help you?"

Myles clasped his perfectly manicured hands behind his back. "I'm actually here on behalf of Her Majesty."

Well, that gave me pause. "Oh?"

"Our beloved royal seamstress is retiring."

My breath stilled, and I was pretty sure the floor beneath me had given way. The royal seamstress, Hanna Marrel, had been at the palace for centuries—a well-known and incredibly talented Fae who'd lived up to her elemental calling with a talent that was unparalleled. Brilliant. Extraordinary.

Retiring.

"Why?"

A bittersweet expression crossed his aristocratic features. "I'm afraid she's decided it's time for her to enjoy the rest of her life. She deserves it after serving the crown for more than a millennium. Which is why the queen has decided to hold a competition for those of you who bear the artist's symbol."

I sucked in a breath as I subconsciously rubbed the Elemental Mark on the skin of my inner left wrist—the mark of an artist. "A competition?"

His delectable mouth twitched at my reaction, and I tried not to focus too hard on that plump bottom lip that I wanted to bite. "Yes. We'll be visiting the shops in the fashion district this week. Queen Neleah will select three designers to compete at Fashion Week for the prize of becoming the royal seamstress." He admired a few dresses on display beside him. "And given your exceptional talent, I'd say you have a very good chance of being selected."

I thought my heart might burst. "You think I have exceptional talent?"

I mean... let's be honest. I *know* I have exceptional talent, but compliments were always welcome.

A knowing grin blossomed on his handsome face as if he could see right through me. "Of course. You're brilliant. Truth be told, I've been an admirer of yours for a long time."

The way he said those words in that deep, masculine voice, with a sensual undertone that snaked its way around my heart—and other places—left me speechless.

And I was *never* speechless.

"So," Myles continued, "I just wanted to pass by so that you might be prepared when she arrives." His focus traveled to the draped back office, and a cheeky grin emerged. "And perhaps you'll ask your friend there to turn down the volume on OnlyFins, lest Her Majesty step through the door while she's indulging."

I swallowed the embarrassment rising in my throat. "Noted."

With a subtle bow, he said, "It was a pleasure seeing you, Aurelio."

He knew my name.

Myles Anthysius knew my name.

As he turned for the door, something stirred in my chest—something I'd only felt with my mysterious lover.

No.

Stop it.

I absolutely would not let this beautiful, regal male climb his way into my thoughts. But as I watched him amble down the streets of the fashion district, casting a final glance and a smirk at me over his shoulder, I couldn't suppress the stir in my chest.

Chapter Two

"H E'S ACROSS THE STREET."

My breath stilled in my chest. "Are you sure?"

"Oh, I'm sure."

Joining Tyla at the front window, we peered across the cobblestone road as we hid safely behind a display. As Myles and the queen chatted while entering my archnemesis's store, I couldn't help but let my stare linger on every curve and broad muscle of his backside.

"He has an ass I'd wear as a hat," I said, a little breathlessly.

Tyla hummed her agreement, eyes glued to said bum.

"But why would he go to *her* shop first?" I scoffed.

Tyla fluttered a hand. "It might have something to do with the fact that Vebulah practically vaulted out of the store to greet them."

Vebulah Vella, my opposite in every way, couldn't possibly come close to high fashion. Her designs were drab. Her colors, dull. I had to wonder how her business managed to stay afloat. Most Atlantians had better fashion sense.

Most Atlantians.

"Desperate."

"So desperate." She glanced at me over a shoulder. "Are you going to speak with him?"

My face contorted. "Heavens no."

"And why ever not?"

"Tyla," I began, placing my hands on my hips, "this is no time to get all gooey-eyed over Mr. Nice Ass."

"Even if Mr. Nice Ass is also Mr. Kind Ass?" she implored with a lift of her perfectly sculpted eyebrow.

"Mr. Kind Ass may be terrible in bed. What... with all the poise and charm. I bet his sexual tastes are incredibly vanilla," I said, while straightening a rack next to the dressing rooms I'd already tended to a hundred times that day.

"Perhaps, but you'll never know if you don't find out."

"I'll leave that particular daydream to the imagination and stick to my masked male, thank you very much."

Tyla sighed with despair. "Really, Aury. How do you expect to continue this annual charade?"

"The same way I've continued my masquerade charade up until this point. I attend the ball in the most elaborate ensemble.

My masked male finds me, and we spend the most incredible night together in nothing *but* our masks—which is slightly tragic, considering how much time I spend on my clothing designs—and then we leave to meet again the next year. Easy peasy. No strings. No commitment. No names."

Tyla folded her arms, casting me an admonishing glare with those midnight-black eyes. "And who's to say your annual lover hasn't found somebody else?"

I gasped. "Take that back."

"I will not."

"Yes, you will."

"No, I won't. If anyone's going to tell you the truth, it's going to be me."

"Well, the truth of that statement is debatable."

Tyla opened her mouth to issue a retort when something caught her eye. "They're coming."

I froze. "Like now?"

"Yes—like now."

"Shit." Searching the room for somewhere to hide, I dove into the dressing room just as the bell echoed throughout the store.

"Greetings, Your Majesty. Secretary," Tyla welcomed them.

"And a good day to you, Bajari," Queen Neleah greeted.

The queen.

In my store.

Within the confines of the small dressing room, I let out a silent scream of excitement.

"And Aurelio?" Myles's smooth tone reached my ears, and my body nearly melted.

"Oh, you must have just missed him. He'll be *so* disappointed that he missed you all. He's been looking forward to it all week."

Goodness. Why not mention that I wanted to suck his dick, while she's at it?

She and I would have to have a little chat about making me seem eager. That wouldn't do.

"I'm sorry to hear that."

Was that a hint of disappointment in his tone?

"Well, feel free to look around. If there's anything you'd like to try on, please let me know."

You'd think Tyla actually worked here and didn't spend her off time hanging out in my store watching OnlyFins for entertainment, given how well she delivered the line.

As the slow sound of footsteps and hangers sliding against metal racks sounded, my back quietly met the dressing room wall, trying with all my might not to make a single sound, which, let's be honest, is quite the task for me.

"My goodness. These garments are absolutely marvelous," I heard the queen say.

"Makes you want to wear clothes in lieu of scales every day, yes?"

"Absolutely." They shuffled to the rack closest to the dressing room door. "Cathan would panic if I brought the entire wardrobe home. But I just might."

Myles's deep chuckle sent a shiver of longing through me. I wanted to hear it again.

"He's exceptionally talented," his remark sent butterflies rippling in my stomach.

"Very talented."

"And incredibly beautiful."

I inhaled sharply, and my hand instantly covered my mouth—my lips moving against my palm, issuing a silent prayer to the goddess that they hadn't just heard me.

"Oh?" the queen asked with interest. "You think he's beautiful?"

"To be sure. He's the most gorgeous creature I've ever beheld."

"My, my. I daresay you sound like you have a romantic interest in the talented designer."

Daresay indeed.

"Can you blame me? There's just..." he paused. "There's something about him."

"I *do* like where this is going," Queen Neleah said cheerfully.

I don't.

I definitely don't.

My heart kicked in my chest, and a tingling sensation bled from my head to my toes as my legs shook with the effort to keep upright against the wall.

"Well, I've seen enough," the queen declared. "I'm good if you are."

"Hmm, I had hoped he'd be back by now," he said, with a longing lilt. I almost leapt out of the dressing room right then. But no. No, no. We mustn't ruin the perfectly good image he had of me with an absolutely batshit crazy version. That wouldn't do. "Nevertheless," Myles continued, "I have a feeling I'll be seeing a lot more of him in the near future, if your fawning over his clothing is any indication."

"My dear Myles. I would never reveal my contestants before I've had time to visit all our wonderful designers." A pause. "But I think you're right," she whispered.

Sliding down the dressing room wall, elation and panic battled within me. The queen loved my work. She thought me worthy, but Myles thought me beautiful. Oh, what a conundrum! My bum became numb as I sat, stewing in my thoughts in the safe confines of the dressing room for what had to be a quarter of an hour before Tyla's hesitant knock drew me from my panic.

"You can come out now," she said. When I didn't open the door, she pulled it open with a timid expression as she beheld me on the floor in all my panicked glory. "What's the matter?"

"The queen thinks I'm talented."

"That's great," she encouraged gleefully.

"She's likely going to select me for the competition."

"That's wonderful news."

"Myles thinks I'm the most gorgeous creature he's ever beheld."

Tyla's mouth rounded in a "o".

My legs gave a brief ache as I sprang from the ground. "No, no. This won't do," I said, breezing past her to my workroom.

"What won't do?"

"Panicking over a male."

"But why are we panicking?"

Whirling around to face her, I said, "Because love and devotion have never led to anything but heartache for me, Ty. I've wasted so much time on males who treated me more as an annoyance or a convenient hole to stick it in. And the Secretary, well, to be frank, I would crush a male like him. He can't handle me."

"Wouldn't it be best for him to decide if he can handle you or not?"

"He can't." A fierce lump formed in my throat. "No one can." Before she could issue a protest, I drew the curtain to my workshop aside. "If you need me, I'll be working on my Starlit Masquerade designs."

"But the masquerade isn't for another few months. You're hiding behind a mask, Aurelio."

Lacking the courage to look at her and see the truth of her words reflected in her eyes, I kept my back to her as I spoke, "Perhaps you're right, but I'd rather stay behind the safe confines of my mask than face the potential of a broken heart."

A moment after the curtain fell, the bell chimed, signaling Tyla's departure. Perhaps I was overreacting. Perhaps, I'd been jaded one too many times. It didn't matter. I'd return to my masked lover. After all, a fantasy is a safe place to hide.

The lie settled in the pit of my stomach as designs flowed across the stark white pages of my sketchbook late into the evening in lonely, blessed solitude.

Chapter Three

TYLA HADN'T BEEN BY the shop in a couple of days—a rarity, to say the least, since she had been by my side nearly every day of my life. Despite their rarity, I didn't like it when we got into disagreements. Tyla's human existence would be over in the blink of an eye, and I wanted to do everything in my power to create happy memories, rather than ones filled with frustration and anger. I sighed heavily from where I sat at the checkout counter, my emotions getting the best of me.

And I *hated* it when my emotions got the best of me.

When the front door chimed, my standard greeting left me, purely out of habit. "Welcome to Enchanted Couture." I couldn't even muster the energy to look up from the garment I was sewing.

"Yes, it is quite enchanting, isn't it?"

On a sharp inhale, my gaze settled on the male with the sensual voice before me. "Secretary," I said, a little breathlessly, though I truly hadn't meant to. But how could I not, when he was dressed so impeccably? His black suit, the color of midnight, pulled snug over every delicious muscle, each button perfectly placed. As he strolled with casual grace to the counter—an envelope in hand and a grin of pure sin on his handsome face—the perfect size of his lean yet muscular thighs moved delectably beneath the fabric of his pants.

Myles Anthysius truly was a fucking marvel, and ironically, he was similarly built like... *Nope. Not going to go there. Thou shalt not compare the two of them.*

"Please, call me Myles."

"I'm sorry?" I said a little dreamily.

His lips pulled up in a smile that could melt iron. "You called me Secretary."

"Oh. Yes. I suppose I did. But I'm happy to call you whatever you'd like."

I'm happy to call you whatever you'd like?
For the love of the goddess, you hornball!

Myles bit his lip, and my focus snagged on the spot where teeth met flesh as he casually handed me the stark white square envelope. "This is for you."

When I took it from his outstretched hand, his fingers gently brushed against mine, and my breath caught. I could have sworn something sparked at our touch, and based on the smoldering look Myles held on me, I didn't think I was the only one feeling... things.

"You have the most extraordinary hands," he remarked, his voice a caress.

"Thank you," I nearly whispered.

"I bet you take care of your entire body in the same manner."

Heat, potent and alarming, rose in my neck and made my designer robes all the more stifling. And words? There were no words. It was the second time this male had left me speechless.

With his heated look held solely on me, Myles strode backward toward the door—hands tucked into the pockets of his perfectly hemmed pants. It was a testament to his unending grace. "I'll be seeing you around, Aurelio."

"B-bye, Myles."

The sound of the bell felt invasive as he exited the shop, but I didn't miss his final glance in my direction as he disappeared from sight.

I expelled the breath I hadn't realized I'd been holding and observed the envelope in my hand. With a furrowed brow, I slid my finger beneath the flap and tore it open. What lay inside sent a flurry of excitement to my belly.

Dear Aurelio Martenos,

It is my honor to invite you to compete for the position of Royal Seamstress. Should you accept, please arrive at the palace no later than one in the afternoon in two days' time. All rules and expectations will be discussed at that time.

I look forward to witnessing your artistry.

Warm regards,

Queen Neleah

My blank stare rose and carried out the shop windows. I'd been invited to compete.

As a well of determination swelled within me, I knew with every fiber of my being, I'd do everything in my power to win.

Shortly after I sent Tyla the good news that I'd accepted the invitation to participate in the competition, she graced me with her presence. I considered my message to be a bit of a peace offering. With her head held high, she glared at me expectantly as she stood in front of my workshop table. A stare-off ensued before I dropped my garment with a hiss of fabric and said, "I have issues with commitment."

Tyla's freshly waxed black eyebrow rose in an arch. "You don't say?"

"It wasn't easy for me to admit that, you know."

"Oh, I know." The corner of her mouth twitched. "I'm proud of you for admitting it."

Crossing my arms over my chest, I tried my best not to act like a petulant faeling. "I just don't want to get hurt."

Tyla pulled up a stool, lowering herself with a softening expression. "How in the world do you expect to find happiness if you don't take the risk?"

"Who says I'm not happy?"

She snorted. "Aurelio, keeping yourself busy doesn't mean that you're happy. I mean, sure. You're thrilled with your business success, but don't try to tell me that when you turn off the workshop lights at the end of the day and head upstairs, there isn't a part of you that longs for something more."

It was a testament to our friendship that she knew me so well. The nights in my apartment above the workshop did tend to get lonely. Sure, I'd go out to dinner with friends and family from time to time, but at the end of a long day, it would be nice to share the "*How did your day go?*" and "*Anything new?*" questions with someone. It would be comforting for *anyone* to just... ask how I was doing. And vice versa. I let loose a sigh. "I've had my heart broken before."

Her head dipped in a nod. "Of course, you have. Rejection is part of the process."

"But what's there to reject? Seriously. I'm fucking fabulous."

"You *are* fucking fabulous. There's no contesting that. But rejection doesn't mean a person doesn't think you're fabulous. It just means they're the wrong fit for you." She tapped her chin in thought. "Think about it like this. Have you ever visited Slay Shoe Shop—"

"Love that fucking shop."

"—and tried on a pair of shoes that you absolutely adored—pined for even—but you tried them on, and the shoe didn't fit right?"

"I hate when that happens," I mumbled.

Tyla pointed at me. "Precisely. Now, knowing my friend Aurelio, I'd bet my Marko Malone's—"

"Blasphemous."

"—that you'd say fuck it. I'm going to buy them anyway. Am I right?"

I shrugged. "Maybe."

"Hmm."

A pause. Then, "Okay, yes. Yes, I would. So, what?"

"So, you'd wear that pair for a while. Even though they don't fit you right, you'd grit through the pain and the blisters, only to sell them to the highest bidder at the exchange in a month."

My face twisted in a grimace. "Of course, I'd sell them. You can't give those away."

"That's not the point."

"Well, I'm hoping you'll get to it soon."

Tyla rolled her eyes with a slight grin. "My point is that had you kept going, had you kept searching Slay's, you'd have found a designer pair that looked just as fabulous and fit just right without wasting your time on shoes that weren't meant for you."

Her words slowly sank in, and my pulse stumbled in my chest. "And you believe my masquerade lover is the pair of fabulous shoes that don't fit?"

"I believe your masquerade lover is the pair of shoes that, while fabulous for a time, eventually begins to cause you pain, while Myles is the pair that looks great and fits just right—the kind you place high up on the trophy shelf of your closet and never let go."

I brushed my thumb across my bottom lip, stewing. "I love those kinds of shoes," I reluctantly admitted.

The smile that bloomed across her face screamed, *Checkmate*. "I know." With an expulsion of breath, she stood from her chair. "I have to be off. My date awaits."

I perked up at that. "New beau?"

She shrugged nonchalantly. "Just having fun. And you know, free food," she said with a wink.

As Tyla departed the shop, my mind drifted and latched onto Myles and the way his hand brushed against mine, and I allowed myself to wonder what they might feel like beneath my scales.

Chapter Four

"N ERVOUS" DIDN'T EVEN BEGIN to describe the feeling that was overtaking my body. I'd upgraded my wardrobe for the occasion, knowing that the minute I stepped into the palace meeting room, my competition would be analyzing every bit of fabric from the stitching to the color choice. It had to be perfect. How else would they surmise who would wipe out the competition?

When I breezed into the room, I stopped short.

Oh, hell no.

My head dipped and retreated as I glared at the designer who definitely shouldn't be there. Vebulah Vella tipped her chin higher at my appraisal, her thin mouth set in a grim line of supreme condescension. And Vebulah, with her lackluster colors and dreadful designs, had zero room to condescend.

"Aurelio. Welcome."

It was only that smooth, deep, silky voice that could have pulled me from my glare fest. It turns out that the owner of said voice was also far more appealing to look at.

By the goddess. He looks delicious.

Myles strode toward me with a smile that had my cock twitching in its pocket, and my breath almost caught when I recognized the outfit he wore. I remembered the day I'd embroidered the design on the heather-grey tunic that paired perfectly with the tailored charcoal pants that fit him like a glove—a creation made with my masked lover in mind. The irony wasn't lost on me.

As he came to stand before me, he reached for my hand and brought it to his luscious lips, pressing a soft kiss upon my skin. "Your choice of ensemble is impeccable, and complements your unending beauty," he said with my hand still held in his, his expression fraught with so much mystery. So much promise.

Despite feeling like I might melt onto the floor, I straightened my spine. "Why, thank you. And may I say, that is a spectacular outfit you've chosen for the occasion."

He gave me a wink.

A wink. Ugh.

Thou shalt think only of masked lover dick. Thou shalt think only of masked lover dick.

"I believe you've met our other designers," he said with politeness, letting go of my hand to motion to the other two occupants in the room. I immediately missed the warmth of his touch.

Giving a respectful nod to Francesca Bonaflyn, a renowned designer whose talent rivaled my own, I said, "Francesca. I'd say I'm surprised to see you here, but then I'd be lying."

A smile lifted her lips. "I am unsurprised as well."

As my gaze slid to Vebulah, my mouth dropped into a firm line. "Vebulah."

"Aurelio."

Myles's attention bounced between the two of us in my peripheral vision, but I didn't dare pull my glare away from my nemesis. I wanted to make my message clear: she was no threat to me, and I would win this thing.

Myles cleared his throat. "Feel free to grab a refreshment. You'll find a bottle of bubbly already open."

"Don't mind if I do." I practically catwalked to the far end of the room, where a server was already pouring a glass for me to enjoy.

"It looks like it's only a competition between you and me, then," I heard Vebulah whisper to Francesca. My Fae hearing could pick up a mouse farting.

Whirling around with my drink in hand, I cast her a feline expression. "I would think twice before you insult Francesca by comparing your less-than-appealing designs to hers."

Vebulah gasped. "Why I—"

"Hello everyone!"

Queen Neleah strode into the room, her shimmering violet mermaid gown hugging every inch of her and complementing her olive skin to perfection. The female responsible for such an impeccable dress followed in her wake. Hanna Marrel assessed us with impassivity. I couldn't tell whether she approved or disapproved of the lineup before her, and my nerves immediately tied themselves in a knot. Her opinion mattered greatly to me. She was, after all, the best designer in all four realms.

Queen Neleah clasped her hands at her middle. "Welcome, designers, and congratulations on your selection for this competition. As you know, our beloved Hanna has decided to retire," she said, glancing momentarily at her with a timid smile. "Therefore, I must find her replacement. I've asked my Secretary to display the three winning looks that had me jumping with excitement. Myles, if you will."

After a brief bow, Myles flicked his wrist, and the wall of water that had been hovering on the far side of the room vanished through the open window, revealing our looks.

Pure, unfiltered rage heated my face.

Of course, she chose the look Vebulah stole.

As I cast the thief a furious glare, Vebulah avoided my gaze. Because she knew the design wasn't hers, and I remember exactly when she stole it.

On one unusual morning, after a night of having one too many drinks at Fae Fling's Book Club, Tyla had fallen asleep at the shop counter while managing the store on her own. After I'd awakened her, I entered my workshop beyond the curtain and found none other than Vebulah Vella standing at my table, flipping through my designs.

"What are you doing?"

Startled, she closed the notebook shut, hiding her hands behind her back. "Just reviewing your designs."

"No one sees my designs."

"Oh. Well, Tyla let me pass."

"The fuck I did," Tyla said from behind me, bleary-eyed.

Vebulah shrugged. "It's not my fault you didn't protest when I asked."

"I was sleeping," Tyla said, face twisted in a sneer.

"Were you?" she asked with mock innocence. "Oh my. Sleeping on the job. That doesn't bode well."

"Get out," I growled.

Vebulah hurried out of the shop so fast that you would have thought a Fire Fae had lit a flame under her ass. It was only when I flipped through my designs that I discovered the torn edges of a page—a page with the design now draped on the mannequin in the palace meeting room.

My *stolen* design.

"These dresses truly are a work of art, and you all should be proud of them," the queen said, none the wiser to my ire in Vebulah's direction. "Now, Myles. Would you review the rules of the competition?"

"Yes, my queen." He stood a little straighter, ever the secretary with his professional poise. "Once again, congratulations to you all. Each of you will be responsible for designing a collection themed around the Starlit Masquerade. Since the occasion celebrates the Above World's Valentine's tradition, you must complete a look that matches the mood of the event. The winning look will be worn at the Starlit Desires Festival by none other than the queen herself."

Queen Neleah beamed with excitement, and I couldn't help but share in it. The designs had already begun to draw themselves in my mind's eye.

"Each of you will be given a budget and free rein to select fabrics exclusively from our queen's personal stores."

I gasped, and the corner of Hanna's mouth twitched. The queen's personal stores were said to house some of the most expensive and divine fabrics from all over the world—fabrics I couldn't wait to get my hands on.

Giving me a knowing grin, Myles continued, "No outside investments or purchases can be made in your collection. They can only come from our Queen's stores and nowhere else. You have until our esteemed Atlantian Fashion Week to complete your collections."

Fine by me.

Why anyone would want fabric from anywhere else was beyond me. However, I did note the look of disappointment on Vebulah's face. A part of me delighted in it.

Was it a petty part of me?

Most certainly.

Did I care?

No. I most certainly did not.

"The winner will be offered a position as the royal seamstress and will enjoy all the benefits and respect the position affords. With that said, are there any questions?" At our silence, Myles motioned to Neleah. "My queen?"

Queen Neleah clapped once in joy. "Excellent! I'm truly excited to see what you all come up with, and I'm sure I'll love every bit of it. Now, your guests are awaiting your arrival in the neighboring room. If you'd follow me."

Filing out of the room, *the* Hanna Marrel slowed her pace until she was next to me. "I couldn't help but notice the filigree design on Miss Vella's dress. It seems to replicate something I've seen on your designs fairly often," she commented with an arched brow.

"Really odd, isn't it?"

"Very." With a knowing expression, she added, "It will be a shame if her collection isn't on the same level."

"I can guarantee you, it won't be."

With a hearty laugh that brought a smile to my face, I walked confidently behind the esteemed designer, feeling seen by someone I looked up to and admired.

And I knew then and there, despite the stolen design, I'd thrive.

I'd win this damn thing.

My eyes immediately found Tyla upon entering; it wasn't hard to spot her, especially with everyone showing their reverence as they entered the luxurious gathering room. Whispers of the Bajari reached my ears as I approached. I gave her a mock bow and pulled her by the hand to the neighboring table, which was littered with champagne and an array of hors d'oeuvres.

"What's got your panties in a twist?" she whispered in a hiss. I nodded toward the far side of the room in answer, and her attention traveled and landed on Vebulah. "Oh, dear."

"Yes."

"Why would she—"

"The stolen design bought her ticket into the competition."

Tyla gasped on a sharp intake of breath. "Please tell me you're joking."

"I wish I were."

"This is all my fault," Tyla said, pinching the bridge of her mesorrhine nose. "If I hadn't had so many drinks at book club—"

"Hey, none of that," I scolded, rubbing her back in a soothing motion. "It's not your fault Drabby Vabby is a thief. She's responsible for her own actions. Besides"—a reassuring smile lifted my lips—"it will make the win all the more satisfying."

Tyla pouted despite my reassurance. "You're sure you're not upset with me?"

"Well, I *could* be upset, but I don't want to provoke the goddess's ire. You are a Bajari, after all."

She swatted my bicep, and laughter erupted from my chest as I tried to block her efforts. "You're impossible."

"But you love me."

"That I do." She grabbed two champagne flutes from the table, handing me one. "To you, absolutely sweeping the competition away."

I clinked my glass against hers. As I sipped my bubbly, an odd sensation of being watched had me scoping the room, eventually landing on those rich brown eyes I'd been growing fond of as of late. A blush crept up Myles's neck at being caught staring, but he quickly recovered and glanced away.

"He's wearing your outfit," Tyla remarked with amusement.

"That he is."

"How curious."

"Nothing to be curious about. It's a great outfit."

"He's been sneaking glances at you ever since you entered the room."

Drawing my observations away from the male in question, I lifted my eyebrow. "Are we going to start this again?"

"What?" she said, bringing her hand to her delicate collarbone in mock innocence. "I'm simply stating that the outfit he's wearing happens to be one of yours, and his attention hasn't left you. You're like a magnet for his eyeballs."

A shrug. "Could be a coincidence."

Her almond-shaped eyes widened a fraction. "Don't look now, but your boy toy is coming this way."

"He's not my boy toy," I hissed, straightening my spine at his approach and feigning indifference while the butterflies in my stomach rioted.

But just as he reached our side of the room—his delicious mouth parting slightly in greeting—Drabby Vabby cut a path between us, close enough to have a casual conversation that I desperately didn't want to have.

"Secretary, such an interesting choice of clothing," she remarked with a hint of judgment. "You'll have to come by the shop. I have far more superior outfits that would blow your mind away."

"And are likely stolen," Tyla murmured behind the rim of her champagne flute.

Vebulah twisted her head toward Tyla. "Bajari, I didn't see you there. How wonderful of you to join us."

That tone.

That fucking tone.

The disrespect was so evident that even Myles cast her a look of consternation.

"The pleasure's all mine, I assure you," Tyla replied with grace. "I wouldn't miss celebrating Aurelio for all the stilettos in Atlantis."

"That's blasphemous," I teased with an expression of gratitude.

"Not when you're worth celebrating. Wouldn't you agree, Secretary?" Tyla asked innocently.

My face heated as Tyla put him on the spot.

Myles, ever the gentleman, cleared his throat. "He *is* worth celebrating." His gaze locked onto mine and stayed there—a tingling sensation coursing through my body at the way he observed me, as if his eyes were penetrating the deepest parts of my soul.

"Actually, I think Councilor Velafyn now owning half the fashion district is something we should all be celebrating."

Our moment of bliss was interrupted by Vebulah's comment. "Pardon me?"

Vebulah smiled with potent glee. "You don't know?"

"Clearly, I do not. What is it you speak of?"

She lifted her champagne flute in the air. "Why, the good Councilor has purchased half the retail space in the district."

She paused, hiding her smile behind her glass. "Including yours."

Behuko Enterprises.

Of course, she'd name it after her distant connection to the throne of Atlantis—one of the only reasons why she's even important. Otherwise, she'd just be another bland Fae female in the realm. I turned toward Tyla and was relieved to find we shared the same sentiment based on her turbulent expression. Melysah's hatred of the Bajari was well known and strongly frowned upon; her particular hatred of Tyla was another thing entirely. To disrespect a Bajari was to disrespect the Goddess Atabey, something Melysah often did. But more importantly, Tyla was a kind soul. There was no reason to hate someone like her. Ire bloomed within me, holding me hostage. I could neither speak nor breathe.

"Well," Myles began, cutting through the obvious tension, "whoever the building owner is, I'm sure it doesn't matter. Both of your shops will thrive." His kind eyes swung to my nemesis. "You are exceptionally talented as well, Vebulah."

Tiny pinpricks of unease crept up my body. Did he not utter those exact words about *my* talent when he came into Enchanted Couture? Something wild and untamed lodged itself in my gut, something that resembled insecurity.

Because, of course. Why would I ever think Myles would only utter something so complimentary to me and me alone? It wasn't like this hadn't happened before.

I can still recall a former lover whispering words of praise in my ear. And I can still hear him whisper those exact words to another male tucked into a quiet alcove at Muse as he was balls deep in the male's ass.

It was silly of me to hold on to any romantic notions about Myles Anthysius. If he could speak those words to Drabby Vabby, who else had he given praise to? Were his other comments just as inauthentic?

"I bet you believe we're all exceptionally talented."

The words were out of my mouth before I could think better of them, and as the hurt flickered in Myles's widened eyes, a wave of vulnerability followed—and that was worse than anything. I'd laid my words down before him like a gauntlet and landed the blow. I could barely breathe. The need to escape had me bowing with a flourish. "I have designs to create. I must be on my way."

Refusing to feel anything but the wall around my heart sliding back into place, I turned my back on Myles's imploring gaze. Whatever passed between Myles and me was an illusion, and I was determined to focus solely on the tasks at hand.

Win the competition.

And settle in the safety of my masked lover.

Chapter Five

OVER THE NEXT SEVERAL days, I dispelled all thoughts of Myles, immersing myself in the creation of my collection for the queen. As the memory of all the beautiful fabrics in the queen's stores drifted through my mind, it became easy to forget. I had so many expensive, luxurious fabrics at my disposal. It was a *dream*. Honestly, I could have slept in that room overnight and been content.

Creativity was my constant companion, with designs flowing onto the page and my sketchbook safely locked up at night, just in case Vebulah got any ideas about visiting again.

"Exceptionally talented, my pretty ass," I murmured for the hundredth time.

The ping from the front door chime reached me in the back of my workshop as I re-sketched a top I'd been working on.

"Oh wow. Those are... just. Wow."

I rolled my eyes for what seemed like the millionth time as Tyla entered the workshop. Goddess help me, I couldn't *not* turn around and see what she had in her hands. A stunning bouquet of yellow tulips—my favorite, damn him—sat perfectly arranged in a simple glass vase that didn't detract from the beauty of the flowers themselves, but complemented them. I let out a groan. "Just place them over there with the others."

Tyla paused, her smile fading, but she did as I asked. I could see her in my peripheral vision glancing over at me with a questioning look. "You're not even the least bit curious what he has to say?"

"I don't have time for words right now."

"But—"

"It likely says the same thing the other notes do, Tyla"—I remembered every word of them despite how hard I tried to feign indifference—"and I simply do not have the time to dwell on him."

Lies.

After a pause, Tyla gave a solemn nod and left the workshop to resume her duties at the counter—duties that included her latest monster smut that featured tentacles. I leaned back from the sketch, appraising the design with a critical eye as the bouquet practically grew legs and walked toward me. At least that's the story I'd tell, because I definitely didn't put down my pencil and stroll to the far side of the room.

Nope. I sure did not.

More lies.

On a long exhale, I plucked the tiny notecard from where it sat nestled within the bright yellow petals, and the words on the card had a pulse of something sharp running through me.

The blush that bloomed on your gorgeous face still lingers in my head.

I crumpled it up and threw it across the worktable. Damn him and his pretty little words. Each notecard was better than the one before it. My attention flicked briefly to the crumbled piece of parchment, then darted away again. With a curse, I picked it up and smoothed out the wrinkles, striding to my notebook and placing it in the back so that it would flatten out. Apparently, I was a bit of a masochist and a sucker for pretty words, because, just like the rest of the notecards, I couldn't bring myself to get rid of a single one of them.

As the day bled into night and the warm glow of the streetlight spilled across the shop, I sat with Tyla at the counter, brooding over all the effort Myles had been putting in. "It's dreadfully romantic," I admitted.

Tyla's oval-shaped face lit up with surprise. "Oh wow. We're able to admit it now, are we?"

I threw the truffle fry I'd been eating onto my plate in frustration. "You know it isn't easy for me."

"I know, my dear," she agreed, wiping her hands daintily with a cloth napkin. "So, what does this mean?"

"I—" My eyes widened on the bouquet just beyond the glass door.

And the gorgeous male hand-delivering them.

"Shit. I'm not here. I am not here."

I fled to the back of the room, and yes, it may have been a little childish, but I hid underneath my worktable as the bell chimed.

"Secretary," Tyla said in amusement at my expense. "So lovely to see you. And those roses. They're stunning."

"Thank you, Bajari."

"Please, call me Tyla."

Please, call me Tyla, I mouthed mockingly underneath the table.

"I'd hoped to give these to Aurelio myself. Is he... is he here?"

The longing in his tone nearly shattered me. I should go to him. Ease his pain. No. No. I should stay safely underneath the table, handsome male be damned.

"I'm afraid he's stepped away and won't be returning for a while. But I'd be happy to hand these to him on your behalf."

A pregnant pause ensued, and I could feel myself heating underneath my designer robe.

"Very well. Thank you, Tyla."

I waited in silence until the door chimed once more.

"You can come out now, because I think this is a bouquet you're really going to want to see."

You would've thought I'd been pricked in the ass—and not in a good way—for how fast I emerged from the workshop. And what I was met with stunned me right where I stood.

The most extravagant bouquet of red roses—the signature color of the Starlit Desires Festival—sat in an intricate vase, so different from the others that had been delivered. But that wasn't what robbed me of my breath. No, it was the sparkling black mask, tightly nestled within the blooming roses, that was responsible for that particular reaction.

The very same mask as my secret lover.

On shaky, webbed feet, I stepped forward and carefully removed the mask from its home within the thorny vines. It was precisely the same: the intricate filigree, tiny diamonds winking along the design, the smooth velvet strap—the one that had brushed against my bare skin at the peak of the masquerade as my lover enacted his plans for me. I shivered at the thought. The mask held a certain familiarity, an opening through the secret door to his heart.

It felt...

Real.

"It came with a note," Tyla said, handing me the notecard with a soft smile.

I took it carefully from her grip, opening it ever so slowly, and the words nearly brought me to my knees.

Come out of hiding and have dinner with me. Please? I long to see all of you. Unmasked.

No. It can't be.

That would... that would change *everything.*

"Tyla?"

"Yes?"

"I think I'm about to faint."

As if on cue, my legs gave way. Luckily, Tyla was quicker with a chair beneath my bum, or else I would've fallen to the floor. She fanned me with an invoice from our latest fabric shipment. "Breathe. Just breathe."

"Am I dreaming?"

"I don't blame you for thinking so. I'd believe I was dreaming, too, if a fine-ass male delivered this many flowers."

"But the mask."

"Yes, there is that. But…" She pursed her lips in thought. "Maybe it's just a coincidence."

"Why do you sound like you're trying to convince yourself of that more than me?"

"Because I am."

"Goddess above." I shook out my hands and sprang from my chair, heading for the front door. "We need to go."

"Okay, but where are we going?" she asked, her stilettos clanking on the tile floor as she followed in my wake.

"We need drinks at Tridentinis."

"I'll never argue with that."

With a flick of the wrist, I locked the shop door behind us and set off down the road to seek refuge amongst the martinis.

Chapter Six

T HE MASK WAS SOFT in my hands as I twisted it this way and that, and I sipped my Shaken, Not Sunken Martini. It was a change from my usual choice, Soused Seahorse, as I was feeling less in the mood for a sugary splurge.

"Why don't you ask him directly?" Tyla queried, twisting the stem of her Liquid Kraken—a delicious dark-rum espresso martini equipped with a chocolate, tentacle-shaped stirrer. Perhaps I'd try that one next. The night was young, and my feelings were strong.

"I can't just walk up to him and ask," I said, aghast. "Imagine what a disaster that would be. Why, hello, Myles. You wouldn't happen to be my masked lover whom I fuck to death every Starlit Masquerade, would you?"

"Technically speaking, you're a power bottom, so *he* fucks *you* to death."

I waved a hand in the air. "You get what I'm saying. I can't just ask. It would make me seem incredibly foolish for pining after some mysterious male. But..." I carefully placed the mask on the tabletop before me. "Do you really think it's him?"

"Actually, yes. I do think it's him." She leaned her elbows on the high-top table. "Think about it. You've had plenty of time to assess your masked lover. His build, his height"—her black eyebrow rose—"his big, beautiful cock. And don't give me that shocked look. Those were *your* words, not mine."

"It was a big, beautiful cock," I murmured into my martini glass.

"So," she continued, "we know his height is similar, yes?"

"Yes, I suppose."

"And what about his shoulders? Broad like your lover's?"

Yes. "Maybe."

"And his figure. What about that?" At my silence, a wide grin formed on her dainty face. "You see? It's not out of the realm of possibilities. Now, you just need to see if his cock is similar, too. Easy peasy," Tyla said with a lift of her drink.

I reclined in my high-backed chair, something heavy—likely the martinis—sinking low into my gut. Myles *was* incredibly similar to my mysterious lover.

"You're realizing I'm right, aren't you?"

"I hate to admit it."

"I know," she said with a wink.

"But... what about the competition?"

She gave her head a tilt. "What about it?"

"Doesn't it look bad that he and I are..."

"Fucking?"

"We're not fucking."

"Dating?"

"We're not doing that."

"Yet."

"Well, yes. But if we were found out, couldn't that be seen as favoritism?"

Tyla huffed a laugh. "He's not the queen, Aury. Besides, isn't he worth the risk?"

I let loose a long, pained sigh because, yes. Myles Anthysius was worth it. "I think I need another round."

We enjoyed another martini... or two, moving on to safer topics before ending our night at Tridentinis. As I strode home on dangerously saucy steps—those martinis are a wonder—I pondered my next move. I could just ignore him completely, stick to my competition, and act nonchalantly about the possibility that he might be my Starlit companion. But no. That wouldn't do. He'd already laid his cards out on the table, and I couldn't look away, certainly not from a male who looked so dashing and had the personality to boot. I let my shoulders slump as I entered my shop. The ruby red roses were a vision in the low, warm light. They truly were perfect. *Damn him.* I carried the vase with me as I climbed the steps to my apartment at the back of the shop, my thoughts a riot. And as I kicked the door shut behind me, the silence that enveloped me was deafening.

Alone.

I felt so *alone*.

Perhaps it was for that reason that I set the bouquet on the table and scribbled a letter to Myles. I'd accept his invitation to dinner, and I'd find out what secrets lay hidden behind his mask.

Chapter Seven

ANXIETY SWELLED WITHIN ME as I waited outside the most extravagant restaurant in all of Borike'n. Tides was an exclusive establishment. You had to make a reservation months in advance to get in, and once you did? Well, you'd better be ready to empty your bank account. The dishes were as extravagant as the restaurant itself. I'd only dreamed of coming to a place like this. I was, after all, a struggling artist, regardless of how high I usually held my chin.

Fake it till you make it and all that.

As I stepped through the tall wooden doors, bracketed by wrought-iron posts with bright green ivy climbing to the top of the jamb, the low hum of music playing from a magicked speaker washed over me and settled in every corner of the restaurant. Each room paid homage to the different Above World seas—the Caribbean being my favorite for obvious reasons—with tones of turquoise and the sounds of rushing water from various waterfalls thoughtfully positioned in the center of every room, leaving me a little breathless.

I was in *Tides*.

Mercy, it was stunning.

The slow, measured clacking of formal shoes drew me from my gawking. I whirled around and wasn't quite done because the male before me took my breath away.

The deep brown strands of Myles's hair were combed to perfection. The low, blue faelights cast his sharp cheekbones in shadow and gleamed across his spotless skin, and that chiseled jaw had me biting my lip. Light from the nearest waterfall flickered in his brown eyes as he took his time dragging his gaze from the top of my black hair down to my sleeveless silver tunic, which hugged the ridges of my chest, then down to my matching trousers, all the way to the tiny diamonds sparkling across my onyx velvet loafers. A warm feeling of satisfaction rolled through me, not only because he was impeccably dressed in a dark blue suit and an even deeper blue button-up shirt with a striped tie I was tempted to grab and yank—perhaps later—but also because his thorough assessment left me with a feeling of radiance.

"You positively take my breath away," he said, but before I could cut in and issue a snarky comeback, he leaned in, and the soft scents of sandalwood and musk overtook my senses.

The same exact scents as my masked lover.

Fuck me.

As he pulled away, he searched my eyes, and my expression must have displayed every internal emotion because the corner of his mouth curved into a shy yet delicious grin. "Thank you for coming."

"Thank you for existing," I breathed. I shook my head. "Sorry, that sounded—"

"Sweet," he cut in, lessening my embarrassment. "It was sweet."

I glanced around the foyer to hide my blush, which surely didn't help. I felt so exposed with Myles. He made me feel things I wasn't ready to face, but I guess I was about to face them anyway.

Myles held his elbow out for me to take. "Shall we?"

Our gazes remained locked as I slid my arm through his. He stood a little straighter, his steps assured as he led us through the main dining room. I felt...

Well, fuck.

I felt special.

I still pondered that feeling as we reached the secluded corner of a nearly empty room. When he pulled out a chair for me, something about that small gesture warmed me both inside and out. I slowly lowered myself, careful not to pull the pristine white tablecloth underneath my legs.

As the hostess placed our menus before us and departed, he leaned back in his chair, his grin doing terrible things to my heart. "Are you enjoying all the flowers?"

I huffed a little laugh. "You'll have to be specific. Which ones? You sent over a dozen."

"I wanted to make a point."

"And what point was that?"

"That you enamor me."

Air stalled in my lungs. The waiter chose that moment to introduce himself to me. Not to Myles, who was greeted afterwards with a "welcome back, Secretary." He proceeded to wax poetic about the chef's special and how it paired perfectly with some type of wine I'd never heard of. Little did either of them know, I was too excited at the prospect of dining at such a fine establishment that I'd already scoped out the menu on my magicked tablet and knew exactly what I planned to order. So, when the waiter asked if we needed a few more minutes to go over the menu, I immediately answered, "No, I'm ready."

The waiter jerked back in surprise. "A male who knows what he wants. Delightful."

"As do I," Myles said, his piercing stare slicing right through me.

"I'll have the chicken fricassee with a garden salad, goddess dressing on the side, please. And a glass of Eliron Chardonnay."

"Make that a bottle, if you will, Rex. And I'll do the same for my meal."

A smile grew on the waiter's face. "Switching it up—that's fantastic. I'll fetch your drinks."

As he slunk away, our attention lingered on each other. I shifted in my seat under his piercing stare. "So."

"So."

"Come here often?"

Bah! What a stupid line.

Judging by the lift at the corner of his lips, he seemed to think so as well. "I come here occasionally," he replied, appeasing me, somehow devouring me without moving an inch.

Is it too hot in here?

I rolled my shoulders. "I suppose I should ask you about your favorite color?"

"Purple."

"Favorite drink?"

"Gin and tonic."

"Nice choice," I complimented.

"I do pride myself on having great taste."

Why did his reply make me want to melt into the floor? *Dearest divine goddess.*

Rex returned with an easy smile and a bottle of wine in hand, uncorking it with practiced ease and providing the usual spiel. I nodded at his script rendition—*buttery notes, full-bodied with a hint of oak*—while Myles's stare never left me. I could feel it, sliding over me.

When Rex finally poured our fill and left the quiet corner of the restaurant, I met Myles's gaze and cleared my throat, the telltale heat creeping up my neck. "I suppose I should tell you a little bit about me."

"No need."

Well, that had my eyebrow lifting. "Oh?"

With practiced poise, he reached forward and took a sip of his wine before divulging, "You were raised in Borike'n, a proper city boy with a well-rounded education. After your Elemental Mark was revealed, you set your sights on design while at Cibao and became a star pupil, excelling in your program and earning the prestigious Delmar Award of Fashion Excellence, the third person in the university's history to receive such an honor. Your parents, Braun and Eytha Martenos, couldn't have been prouder. They still tell their neighbors all about your accomplishments where they live in the outskirts of Calichi, enjoying their formative Fae years."

With a parted mouth, I regarded him in question. "My, my. Been stalking me, have you?"

The epitome of calm casualness, he rested his chin in his palm. "I make it my business to investigate everyone who comes within a hair's breadth of the palace and our queen."

"How very thorough," I murmured as I took a sip.

"Interesting debacle in college." An amused expression glimmered across his handsome face. "Caught skinny dipping with the polo team?"

A shrug. "I'm owed some level of fun."

"I'm sure it was," he teased.

"Enough about me," I said, placing my wine glass on the pristine white tablecloth. "What about you? Are your parents here in Borike'n?"

His expression faltered a bit. "My father is beyond the Veil, but my mother is alive. Doing well for the moment, but missing her bondmate terribly."

I shook my head a bit. "I'm sorry. I didn't mean to pry."

"I don't mind. I like sharing things with you."

Our gazes collided, and once again a flicker of awareness traveled down my spine, like we'd known each other far beyond the competition and the beautiful, overflowing bouquets that screamed of promise. I shifted in my seat. "It must be terrible to lose a bondmate. Perhaps that's why I plan on never having one."

You would have thought I shot Myles in the chest by how visibly he jerked at my remark. He recovered and reached for the wine bottle, refilling our glasses. "And why ever do you plan on never having one?"

"I don't know," I confessed, pursing my lips in thought, "I guess I've been alive too long, had my heart broken too many times to believe in the notion of a bondmate. I apologize if that was too honest."

Myles dashed a hand. "No, no. You have no need to apologize. I value your honesty. But I just wonder if perhaps..."

He paused a moment, fidgeting uncharacteristically in his chair.

"Perhaps?"

"I just wonder if perhaps you're shutting yourself off because you've allowed an unworthy suitor to rob you of your happiness. If you turn away something as beautiful and sacred as a bondmate—someone the goddess has chosen for you—are you not letting the unworthy suitor win?"

Stunned.

I was completely and inevitably stunned into silence.

"Besides," he continued, when it was clear I couldn't form words to issue a clever retort, "I've heard the bond between mates can be very… sensual." His soothing, smooth voice dropped into dangerous territory. "Consuming. Like breathing fire into one's body and soul to the point of madness, that when they come together, something… magical happens."

"You don't say?" I rasped.

The shades of brown in his irises seemed to shimmer with desire, and his sultry expression had me desperate to be his dirty little Fae slut in the best way possible. I wanted to crawl underneath the table and unzip his flawlessly tailored pants with my teeth to find what I knew lay beneath the fabric.

"I'd bet if you were to find your bondmate," he continued, none the wiser to my slutty unraveling, "your heartbeat would kick a rhythm in your chest, and perhaps your cock might stir uncontrollably in its pocket."

My breath hitched.

"Perhaps your breath might hitch," he said with a surprisingly sly smile.

Well, shit.

It just may be that Myles Anthysius wasn't so vanilla after all. I was a hot second away from begging him to take me out of that fancy restaurant and twist me up like a pretzel, but with the arrival of our dinner, the mouthwatering smells diverted my attention. Plus, I had my virtue to think about.

Just kidding.

I had no virtue.

But I did have a rule. No sex on the first date. And Myles was making that rule increasingly difficult right now.

As I snapped my napkin into my lap, I tried my best to suppress my smile. "Well, well, Secretary. It appears your mask of propriety is slipping."

Myles grabbed his fork and sliced the tender chicken with his knife as he said, "All masks must come off at some point." His heavy stare, full of all kinds of meaning, lifted to meet mine.

And with that declaration, Myles placed another chink in the armor around my heart.

After having our fill of the most decadent wine and extraordinary food—all without a single complaint about the cost from Myles—he and I sat in that quiet corner of Tides talking about the past. We discussed how he came to be Secretary, his lineage, and the role his family played with the royal one, as well as an exchange of our different philosophies. His perspective was that he preferred to focus on the good in others, while I tended to mouth off to mean people, good side be damned. All in all, the dinner had been carefree; enjoyable even.

Incredibly surprising.

Myles was a mystery I found myself wanting to unravel in every way.

When Rex came by to inform us that the restaurant was closing for the evening, we both shared a look of amusement. We hadn't even noticed the time. Even now, as we strode down the streets of Borike'n toward my shop, the roads were understandably quiet due to the late hour.

When the front door of my shop came into view, an oddly sad feeling settled over me, knowing our date had come to an end.

"Thank you for such a lovely evening," he said lowly as if not to wake my neighbors.

Turning toward him, a smirk lifted my lips. "Sorry to make you work for it."

"It was no work at all," he replied immediately.

I pitched a shaky thumb over my shoulder. "Nightcap?"

He huffed a little laugh. "No, I think I'll pass. The night is getting late."

I couldn't help but feel rejected, and it must have shown on my face because he immediately brought a hand to my cheek, cupping it gently. "Don't take offense." He leaned in further, and I lost my ability to think; his scent—sandalwood with a hint of musk—consumed me. "It's just... that when I do come up for a nightcap, I plan to take my time." Myles brought his lips to the curve of my neck, his breath tickling my skin. "I want to find out which parts of you elicit desire—unfiltered desire—so that I may bring you pleasure again and again and again."

"Goddess," I whispered.

Myles's breath taunted my lips. "Goddess indeed."

His mouth found mine in the most eager, beautiful, and ravishing kiss I'd ever experienced. We fused together like two pieces of a long-lost puzzle. The way his hands curled into my hair, holding me to him, the way his tongue melded with mine—it had my toes curling and my dick aching to be set free. Pressing me into the wall beside the door, wicked heat pooled in my cockpocket as he slowly thrust his very sizeable, hard length into mine. I braced myself with the lapels of his jacket, needing to keep him with me, needing him to consume me.

"Myles," I moaned.

"Mmmm, the way you say my name. I want to bottle it so that I can stroke myself, listening to your voice." He pecked soft kisses across my jawline until he reached my ear. "I plan to fuck that pretty little ass until it's the only name that falls from your lips for eternity."

I whimpered.

Whimpered.

And I *never* whimper.

Slowly, Myles pulled away, absolutely enthralled with one another. He straightened his lapels, clasping the button of his jacket that must have come undone at some point while I was clawing at him like a needy beast. As if I needed cause to melt even further into the floor, Myles reached up and drew a finger down my cheekbone almost reverently, as if memorizing every detail—his soft touch leaving a stream of goosebumps in its wake. "I'll be in touch." And words simply wouldn't form as he leaned in, giving me one last, beautiful, chaste kiss that I'd remember for the rest of my long days.

As I watched Myles walk toward the palace, I studied him for a minute. If you had told me Myles Anthysius would utter such naughty words, kiss me to the point of fainting the way he did, and leave me wanting him so badly that I was tempted to stroke myself right there in front of my shop, I would have said you're a goddess damn liar.

But here I was, doing all of those things.

Well, minus the stroking-in-the-streets part. I did have some decency. That certainly didn't stop me from finding my pleasure later that evening while replaying his naughty words.

Chapter Eight

MOVIE NIGHT AT TEMPLE Park was an Atlantian staple, and if you hadn't been, you truly hadn't experienced life. As was tradition, a dome elemental—the Fae with the magical calling to create and maintain a protective dome over the realm of Atlantis—cast a projection over the entire park, as if everyone present were part of the movie itself. Patrons could either bring a blanket and lie on the cool grass while they watched or rent a private cabana for a more comfortable and intimate evening.

I don't have to tell you which one Myles chose for our second date. After a long, grueling few weeks packed with designing, cutting, stitching, and dyeing, I was desperate to take a break. When his note had arrived with yet another stunning bouquet of lilies, I let a smile spread across my face. I felt as giddy as a schoolboy with a very terrible crush.

Meet me at the south side entrance. We're cabana number forty-seven, the note beside the baby's breath had read.

I summoned the courage to reply directly to him on my tablet, something that had occurred very few times since our last date, and that incredible kiss that still lingered in my memories.

You didn't say please.

His reply was almost instant.

Would you please do me the honor of meeting me in Temple Park so that I may spoil you while we watch A Midsummer Night's Dream?

I didn't even want to see my face and how wide I was smiling for fear of embarrassment.

Well, when you ask so nicely.

"You must be getting some good dick," Tyla said from the doorway of my workshop.

Placing my hands on my hips, I cast her an affronted look. "I'll have you know that we haven't slept together, thank you very much."

"But if he's your masked lover, then you've been sleeping together for decades," she pointed out with a saucy smirk.

"But we don't know if he *is* my masked lover, so that doesn't count."

She quirked an eyebrow. "And you haven't bent over for the unmasked, very delectable, 'two-scoops-of-ice-cream of an ass' version of him? I don't believe it."

I shrugged. "Believe what you want then."

Her eyes went wide. "Ooooh. You've got it bad then."

"I've got what bad?"

"It."

"What's *it*?"

"You know, the love bug."

I set my tablet on the workshop table, where I pretended to find something extremely interesting. "Don't be so dramatic."

Tyla brought her hand to her collarbone, feigning innocence. "I'm not being dramatic. I'm simply stating that you look all doe-eyed over there."

"I'm not *doe-eyed*," I insisted, even though we both knew it was a lie.

Tyla plucked the note from its home amongst the flowers, her eyes going wide. "Oh, how romantic! He rented a cabana for you at Temple Park."

"Oh, stop." Snatching the note from her hand, I gave her an exasperated look that masked the smile wanting to emerge. "Don't you have somewhere to go where hordes of people can fawn over you, oh holy Bajari?"

"Actually, I do. I've got a double date."

I felt a crease form on my brow. "A double date?"

"Yes," she said, lifting the vase of lilies from the table.

"With who?"

"With not one, but two males. For me and me alone."

"That's not technically a double date."

"It is to me," she said, winking. "I must be off now."

"Hey, where are you going with my flowers?"

She glanced over her shoulder with a cheeky shrug. "You've gotten enough flowers. Besides, I want to look at them and play make believe that I'm the one getting dicked down by the hot ass Secretary."

"He hasn't 'dicked' me down," I quipped.

"Yet."

And with that, Tyla left me alone with my thoughts in the back of the shop. I couldn't blame her for not believing me—it was unbelievable to me that Myles and I had only kissed. Most males... well... they tended to take advantage of the situation, and truth be told, sometimes the dry spell can linger. Better to scratch the itch. However, sometimes I wondered what it would feel like to have a male's undivided attention, for him to see me for who I really was, for a male to get to know... me. Truly. And now that Myles was... what's the word? *Wooing* me? I was utterly terrified to find out where this would go. Terrified...

Yet intrigued.

It was a curious position I'd never found myself in before.

Later that evening, as the dome sun slowly set over Atlantis and the early evening sky bled from beautiful shades of pink and orange to a lovely violet hue, I reached the south side of the park, where the area was roped off for the cabanas. I opened my mouth to provide my name, but the security guard ushered me through. "This way, Mr. Martenos."

Oh. Okay, then.

Following in the wake of the burly security guard, he led me down a stone pathway to a quiet cabana that was a little separate from the others. A smile breached my lips when I beheld the male standing in front of it. Myles looked positively dashing, opting to embrace his Water Fae form this evening—he'd fashioned his scales into a sleeveless shirt with a flared collar. Casual. Cool.

Mouthwatering.

His open, unabashed perusal swept over me, my cock already hardening beneath my scales despite the millisecond I'd been in his presence.

I really need to get it together.

When my gingerly steps brought me before him, Myles reached out and slid his palms along my face. A gasp left my lips as he pulled me to his luscious mouth, warm and soft against mine. I couldn't help but breathe a sigh of borderline need. Pure, lustful, slutty need.

What's wrong with me?

Slowly pulling back, he studied my face with something I wasn't quite ready to place. "Hello, darling," he said above a whisper.

His term of endearment zinged right to my heart—a feeling of belonging, of being adored, settled over me. The corner of my mouth lifted. "Hello to you, too handsome."

Very aware of the hand at the small of my back, he motioned to the cabana with the other. "I took the liberty of packing a light snack. Some wine as well."

"That sounds lovely."

I lowered myself into the cabana, my body sinking into the plush cushions as I settled against the mountain of pillows at my back and watched Myles expertly open the bottle of wine. "So, do you often come to movie night at the park?"

"Not as often as I would like," he answered, handing me my glass of wine. "If I do, I usually plop down a blanket on the main lawn."

"You know, a blanket would have been enough for me."

"Oh, I know." Myles effortlessly climbed onto the cabana cushion, but instead of settling next to me, he moved the pillows at my back aside and settled in behind me, encompassing me in his warmth. How he managed to do that without spilling a drop of his wine was a testament to his grace. His exhale brushed against my ear. "But you deserve to be spoiled."

My lungs stuttered as he placed a kiss on my neck. "You keep that up, and we'll never make it to the end of the movie."

He chuckled against my skin, his lips pulling away, and I immediately regretted saying anything at all. "Fair enough. Hungry?"

"Not for anything you have in your picnic basket, I assure you."

That drew a deep laugh that rumbled against my back. "Well, if you get hungry for whatever is in the picnic basket... or out of it... I'm happy to oblige."

How in the world was I going to make it through this movie without climbing him when he said stuff like that? *Goddess save me.*

The effort not to do so lingered as I lay in his arms. Every slight caress—his finger trailing along my arm, leaving a riot of pebbled skin in its wake—sent an undeniable ache coursing through my body that beckoned obsession. It stirred a feeling within me that I couldn't quite put into words. There was something quite thrilling about being held by this male, being cared for and tended to, that felt almost... right.

It was an act of the goddess not to jump his bone when the wine and cheese were gone and our glasses had been set aside. Even as the movie credits spilled across the projection dome, I refused to get up and nestled into Myles's warmth, unwilling to let go.

It wasn't until the movie was long over and conversations outside the cabana had died down that I turned in Myles's arms, about to ask if we should finally leave, but when I met the hungry and incredibly potent look piercing straight into my soul, my limbs locked up of their own accord.

"I'll be leaving for the evening, Secretary," the security guard's voice called from the cabana opening. And still, Myles did not pull his eyes from mine.

"We're going to stay a while, Vel. Thank you."

The slight shuffle of the guard's steps across the pathway faded as Myles brushed a lock of my hair back into place. "Stunning. You are absolutely stunning."

When the corner of my mouth twitched and a prickling heat bloomed on my neck, I hardly recognized the confident designer I'd been before I stepped into the cabana, before Myles came pummeling into my life. He had a way of dismantling me until I was nothing but a shy, smitten male before him. "I bet you say that to all your conquests."

His elegant finger slipped under my chin, lifting it so that his next words might bore further into my soul. "First, you are not a conquest. You, darling, are a journey—one I am desperate to take."

I swallowed past the lump in my throat.

"And two," he continued, his thumb brushing across my cheekbone. "I'm only capable of saying such things to you, the male for whom all the world appears as a god personified, cut from the stone the goddess has supplied so that all the realms may witness his beauty."

Words failed to form on my tongue. They were deemed otherwise unnecessary as Myles slowly brought his soft lips to mine, the warm press of them robbing me of all other thoughts except him. When his fingers slid across the back of my neck, gripping me with a gentle possessiveness, I submitted to the growing feeling that was consuming me. I completely lost myself in him—the way his tongue slowly slid into my mouth and tangled with mine, the way he pulled me closer into his strong, hard body. There was a slight dominance in his touch that, while entirely overwhelming, felt...

Right.

Something awoke within me, and I slid my arms around him as he lay down on the velvety cabana cushions, pulling me beside him. Our kiss turned from passionate to ravenous in the blink of an eye. Wild. I was completely wild for him, absorbed in every movement of his body, every caress of his hand down my back. Kneading. Massaging.

Possessing.

I moved, peppering kisses down his deft jawline and licking my way down his neck, a sharp inhale rattling through him.

"Relio," he breathed.

As my tongue continued its assault on his neck, I pondered the notion that my masked lover couldn't have breathed my name the way Myles had, because he couldn't well and honestly know who I was. I quite liked the term of endearment. The Starlit Masquerade was one night. But Myles? Myles could be *every* night, with "Relio" spoken in reverence. And I found I wanted that. Some deep, suppressed part of me truly wanted that.

Myles's hand coasted down my spine, leaving goosebumps in its wake, while his other hand reached for something within the picnic basket I failed to see in the dark. When he crested the swells of my ass, he tapped a finger upon the scales there. "Drop your scales, my pet," he demanded.

Shamelessly gawking at this glorious male, I obliged his will. My scales retreated, and my throbbing cock pressed against his scaled bulge still hidden in his cockpocket. I wanted to feel every part of him, explore every inch, but as I remained locked in his embrace, I found myself at his mercy and content to stay there. His deft fingers cut a path across my lower back and settled between the curves of my ass, brushing against my tight ring, and a desperate sound of pure, undeniable need left me. My hips rubbed harder against him, and the corners of his lips pulled up in a taunting smirk.

"There, there, my little minx," he murmured, grazing my jaw. "So desperate for my cock."

Fuck! That mouth! "Yes," I whispered, unable to deny it. When two of his very skilled fingers slick with the lube he must've procured from the picnic basket dipped inside me, I whimpered in anticipation, thrusting against his length. His lower half still remained scaled, and it edged me, drove me to complete and utter madness. Given the devilish smirk on that gorgeous face, I deduced it was his intention. I wanted to feel his dick against mine, craved the feel of him. "Please drop your scales," I begged. "Please."

Myles caressed my cheek with the thumb of his free hand. "Who am I to deny you anything?"

"Oh, goddess." The brush of his scales retreating against my raging length nearly sent me over the edge. Pumping his fingers in and out of my ass while pressing me harder into him wasn't helping me to keep from spilling all over his tight abdomen—his thick girth rubbing against mine in the most tantalizing way. Control slipped from my grasp, and I became a prisoner to his touch, a willing participant to his seduction.

"Look at you unravel for me," he murmured in a gravelly tone. "Oh, the things I have planned for you." As he pressed the heel of his palm harder into my lower back, he swallowed my moan. I could hold back no longer. "Myles."

"That's it, my sweet. Spill your seed on me."

Ropes of hot, pearly cum spilled forth upon the plains of his tight stomach. Erotic. It was entirely erotic.

And I was loving every moment of it.

"Fuck. You look so stunning when you come." His hips rubbed against me in a frenzy, spreading the evidence of my desire between our stomachs. His mouth dropped open. "I can't—"

When Myles threw his head back in a heady growl, I felt I might come again at the sight. *Goddess, save me.* The prominent Adam's apple, the way it bobbed on his enticing neck as he grunted his release. I knew right then and there that I was in deep, deep shit.

Pulling his head up with hooded, mahogany eyes full of exhaustion and lust, Myles smiled at me with something akin to happiness, something akin to a male who'd struck gold. And as he summoned his water magic, taking great care to clean me thoroughly in all the places, I let myself be swept away in it all, knowing I was unable to stop the train that had departed from the station of my heart.

All aboard, I guess.

Chapter Nine

SINCE OUR STEAMY CABANA encounter, I'd found my thoughts drifting to Myles—his body pressed against mine, his gentle handling of my most intimate places. Myles Anthysius had handled me with the skill of someone who knew every inch of my body, and given the mask that had accompanied his invitation to dinner, along with the striking similarities between them... well, it was damn near impossible not to compare the two. Especially when it came to... ahem... certain departments in the lower region. My face heated as those images swirled in my mind and didn't stop, even when a messenger from the palace hand-delivered a note from the male in question. I quickly tore open the ruby red seal and scanned the contents with a grin.

Dearest Aurelio,

I wondered if you might want to join me on a bit of a diplomatic mission tomorrow morning. Will you be my guest?

Affectionately Yours,

Myles

The royal messenger didn't have to wait long for my reply. In truth, my response took less time to write than it did to figure out whether I should don my scales for the royal event—whatever it was—or sport my designer robe, which was, in my opinion, always in fashion. Deciding on my scales with a pop-collar, sleeveless design, I found myself at the address the messenger had provided, my brow furrowed. The tall sandstone building with rows of arched windows reached up to the dome of the sky and loomed over me.

"There you are," his sensual voice said, my confused expression morphing into one of delight at the sight of Myles, who looked incredibly dignified and gorgeous beyond words.

How did I get so lucky?

His fresh, musky scent washed over me as he leaned in, placing a chaste kiss upon my cheek. "Thank you for meeting me here."

I coughed and tipped my head toward the building to hide my blush. "It's the human children's hospital."

Myles uncharacteristically rocked on his feet. "That it is."

"And... uh..."—I pointed over my shoulder—"this is your diplomatic mission?"

"That it is."

"I see," I replied slowly, feeling a little uneasy.

Myles tilted his head. "Is this okay?"

I fluttered a hand. "Of course, it's okay. Why wouldn't it be?" I quickly recovered. I had assumed I'd be presented before his colleagues or peers. I hadn't expected to be presented before a bunch of crotch goblins—no offense to the little humans. I was sure they were lovely. Truly.

After a beat, he motioned to the front door. "Shall we?"

Wringing my hands, I entered through the door that Myles held open for me into Atlantis's premier hospital—a hospital well known for rehabilitating young human children when disease had spread in their quarters. Coral Refuge Children's Hospital had been around nearly as long as Atlantis. In secret, it had introduced technology so advanced to the Above World that humans were nearly cured of every known disease. But as the last Ice Age swept away those who remained above, so too did the technological advancements that the Atlantians had introduced to the humans. And so, the cycle started anew. Although the current era of humans seemed to have put up a fair bit of resistance to the technologies we've tried to introduce; something Queen Neleah has been very vocally disappointed about.

The tips of Myles's fingers brushed against my forearm and slid to my palm, threading themselves through my hand. I glanced down at where we were joined before recovering with a smile I couldn't hide. Here we were in public, and he was making a statement, his brown eyes brimming with something akin to pride.

I was with him.

Something warm burst into my stomach, skipping around.

Myles led us to the cancer unit of the hospital, and my steps faltered. It was one thing to visit the children's facility, but when the playroom was packed to the gills with children, I began to examine my life choices.

"Is something wrong?" Myles asked with an amused smile.

"No, nope. Nothing at all."

His hands slid around my waist and settled on my lower back. "I know you're lying."

"Am I?"

"You are."

"And how do you know I'm lying?"

"Because your nose does this little twitch," he said, his face alight with knowing. "It's actually quite endearing."

I immediately reached for my nose with a scowl. "I didn't even know I was doing that."

He laughed, and it immediately put me at ease. "Relax, Relio. You're not afraid of a few children, are you?"

I ran a finger along the scale of his pec, refusing to look at him. "No, it's not that. It's just... I haven't really been around many children," I confessed. "What if they don't like me?"

Myles's hands left my lower back and cupped my face, and this relaxed part of him—the part that made me feel like he was just this way for me and me alone—had my heart soaring. "All you have to do is be yourself and they will love you." My mind went fuzzy when he leaned in and kissed me chastely. "Come on."

With his hand in mine once again, Myles led us into the room, and every tiny human eye was upon us—some with curiosity, others with wonder.

"Myles!" one of the young boys shouted from the back of the room.

He was in Myles's arms in an instant, with Myles spinning him around in a circle. "Oh my goddess, Vick. You need to stop growing." He placed the little boy on the ground as he beamed up at him.

"Nurse Naya says I've grown a whole inch in the past month," Vick said with no short amount of pride.

Myles rubbed the blond hair of Vick's head. "I can tell."

It was then that Vick noticed me, a questioning expression on his young, boyish face.

With the corner of his mouth lifting, Myles motioned to me. "Vick, meet Aurelio—one of Atlantis's top designers."

"*The* top designer," I corrected as I held out my hand to the human boy. "It's a pleasure to meet you."

Vick took my hand with a frown. "Designer? Like of human clothing?"

"That's correct."

"I knew it!" came a voice from the other side of the room. Apparently, I'd garnered the attention of a young girl, no more than ten or eleven years old, with wide blue eyes, and a hand slapped over her mouth.

The Fae standing behind her, from her vantage point on a swiveling chair, gave her an amused look that the little girl couldn't see. "Do you know him, Albie?"

When Albie twisted in her chair to cast the female an incred-ulous look, I had to bite my lips to stifle my laugh. "Know him? I know every single piece of clothing he's ever made in a youth size ten." She pointed at me. "He's the owner of Enchanted Couture. Everyone knows who Aurelio Martenos is." Her gaze swung my way. "What's he doing here?"

Myles hid his laugh behind his hand, and I seized the oppor-tunity to bow to my little fangirl with a flourish. "I'm here for you, actually," I said.

"Me?" she squealed.

I sauntered over to her chair. "That's correct. I heard you were a fan, so I thought I'd stop by and say hello." I glanced at the Fae female behind her and gave her a wink. It was only when I noticed her hand coasting over the crown of the young girl's head that I understood why she was there. The Fae female, a healer, was holding the young girl's hair in place to prevent it from falling out due to the treatments. I'd bet she had already taken care of Albie's nausea before casting her latest spell. They really did fantastic work for the children.

When a younger group of girls slowly shuffled over to Albie's chair with curious looks on their cherubic faces, I suddenly realized I was the belle of the ball. I glanced back at Myles, who'd already started helping the young boys in the corner of the room assemble a train set around the perimeter. I cleared my throat, bringing my attention back to the wide-eyed little girls.

"So," I began, clapping my hands. "What should we do to-day?"

"I want to learn how to sew!" Albie said.

"I want to make a dress!" another girl yelled.

"Teach me how to sketch a design. Pleeeeeeaaaaase!" yet another request.

An idea formed in my head, and I smiled at my little entourage. "If that's what my new friends want to do, then that's what we'll do."

I whipped out my tablet and immediately sent Tyla a message.

"That's a magnificent design, Jade," Tyla encouraged, her dark eyes perusing the drawing that the young girl had sketched in the new notepads we gifted to the group. "I love the skirt."

Jade's little cheeks grew red from the compliment, and something stirred in my soul at the sight. When Tyla arrived, the children gasped as the Bajari strolled in, carrying leftover fabrics I had stored in the back of the shop, along with brand-new sketch pads and pencils that I had Tyla pick up from the craft store. My little entourage of four girls and one curious boy named Adym, who'd gleefully left Myles and the boys to their train set to join us in sketching and sewing, was blissfully working away. Albie bit her lip in deep concentration, trying to thread a needle through the hole of a button. Witnessing her commitment to learning throughout the afternoon left me with a sense of contentment I hadn't known I was capable of. The children were truly extraordinary.

As my musings carried my glance to Myles—the train track of the playset they'd been assembling nearly completed around the room—I admired the patience he had with them, the encouragement he gave at every turn. And the endearing way they hung on Myles's every word had me longing for something I'd never considered before.

Stability.

Something so different from what I'd been used to with the mysterious masked male.

The comfort of knowing I'd come home to Myles at the end of a long workday at the palace, after assembling the most exquisite collections for the queen. And perhaps the little squeals of a faeling who would exude sheer happiness at the arrival of his papas coming home. There were plenty of surrogate mothers in Atlantis who'd volunteer for the chance to provide a faeling, although I'd never had a reason to consider it before because...

Well...

I'd never seen a male who looked as elated as Myles did while assembling a train set, or someone I cared to envision a future with. Now? I found I wanted this thing blooming between us; this future I never ever thought was possible.

"Someone's got bondmate fever." Albie's little voice cut through my illusions.

My head snapped to the little girl, casting her a disbelieving look. "Bondmate fever?" I questioned, my voice pitched a little higher than usual.

"Yeah, bondmate fever." She pulled her thread through the other buttonhole with a satisfied smile. "You know. When bondmates can't keep their eyes off each other before they formally present themselves at Guake'te."

Tyla snorted, and I scowled briefly in her direction.

"I have no idea what you're talking about, young lady."

With an arched brow and an expression beyond her ten years, Albie nodded toward the corner of the room. I turned toward the handsome Secretary, and something seemed to pass between us as his eyes met mine.

Holy shit.

Was Myles my...

"Oh no," Tyla breathed. "Don't do that."

"Do what?" Albie asked, unaware of the panic coursing through my veins.

A firm grip on my chin had me turning my head to meet Tyla's determined face. "Breathe."

Jade started fanning me with her sketch pad, her expression concerned. "Is he alright?"

"Yes, my dear," Tyla said with an assurance I didn't feel at that moment. "Just a little overwhelmed."

I glanced at Myles and scratched the center of my chest as a sensation tingled against my skin. A very real, very plausible thought rolled through my mind.

Was Myles my bondmate?

That question lingered and looped on a reel as the day with the children came to an end. With Tyla off to receive a complimentary massage from boyfriend number five, it was just Myles and me strolling through the streets of Borike'n as we made our way back to the shop. Myles was just as quiet and contemplative as I was. My mind was a mess of confusion and fear. I'd been so preoccupied with my thoughts that I had hardly noticed Myles stop at a storefront several paces away.

My storefront, apparently.

With a twisted grin, Myles closed the distance between us. "What's on your mind?"

His features were entirely disarming, which did nothing to help my nerves. "Today was…"

"Too much?" he provided.

I winced. "No, the children were lovely. *You* were lovely with them, and it had me wanting… things, contemplating things I'd never thought of before."

He dipped in my line of vision, ever the patient soul. "And is it bad? To want those things?"

"No, not bad. Just…" Exciting. Exhilarating. I said none of those things. "It makes me a little nervous."

Understanding dawned across his face. "You know, it's quite all right to want those things, yes?"

"Is it?" I asked, my voice laced with vulnerability.

Myles stepped even closer until his hands looped around my waist, pulling me toward him. "Yes, it's great to want those things." Those beautiful brown eyes searched me, sending a surge of emotion quivering in my chest. "And it's okay to want those things with someone you care about. Deeply." He brushed the tip of his nose against mine. "It's also okay to pause and take our time. We have the benefit of a long life, do we not?"

His words immediately put me at ease. He was right, of course. Whatever I was feeling, nothing had to be decided right this second. Whatever this was, we had time to explore it.

I brushed my hands over his biceps, his muscles firm and warm against my palms. "Thank you."

"Anytime," he replied with a smile that could melt iron. "Now, make sure to be ready by nine tomorrow evening."

I jerked back slightly with an arched brow. "What's tomorrow evening?"

Myles leaned in, his nearness curling around me, and I almost forgot my question entirely. "I thought perhaps I'd take you out dancing, since I know how fond you are of it." The space seemed to electrify between us. "And maybe this time you'll enjoy a dance without the mask."

Myles captured my gasp in a ravenous kiss that had the question, *What did you mean by that?* flying firmly out of my mind. Tongue taking and twisting with mine in a desperate dance. When he retreated slightly, my mind was muddled, my breathing erratic.

With one last long, lingering kiss, Myles stepped back and issued a wink. "See you tomorrow, darling."

And I stood there, unable to move, ogling the curves of his perfect backside as he disappeared into the crowd of the bustling Fashion District.

Chapter Ten

As we approached the entrance of Pearl—Atlantis's esteemed club where invitations were a requirement—my heart beat a steady rhythm in my chest. It seemed to dance to the pulse of the music pouring out of the ornate windows, the wooden shutters open to the street below, which revealed the dark room with flashing lights within. The shadows carefully hid the debauchery I knew awaited us once we crossed the threshold.

"Ready?" Myles asked, his breath cresting across the shell of my ear as he held me from behind while we waited for entry.

I twisted in his arms with a sly smirk. "As I'll ever be." The need that hummed within had me closing the distance between us. I licked the seam of his lips and captured his bottom lip, sucking it with a soft plop that had his stare morph into one of hunger and desire.

I let loose a squeal of surprise when he swatted my ass.

"Minx."

"Only for you."

My eyes instantly widened.

I don't know why I said it. We'd never discussed exclusivity, never uttered a word about it, and as his face lit up with something like surprise, I wondered if my declaration had been too bold.

"Move it along!"

The bouncer's call snapped us out of our lust-filled trance, and Myles promptly handed him the invitation for the evening. With the bouncer's bored perusal of the gold flinted card, he promptly let us inside, Myles's hand threading through mine. Something about the way he led me through the crowd to the second floor set my heart alight. His gaze swept over anyone who glanced in my direction with a blend of pride and possession, making it very clear that I was his and his alone. I couldn't help but squeeze his hand in assurance.

The second floor, which overlooked the dance floor below, was less crowded and reserved for those with special invitations. It didn't shock me in the least that Myles had procured the all-inclusive kind, complete with endless drinks.

"VIP section, huh?" I called over the music.

He leaned into my ear, and goosebumps broke out against my skin. "Only the best for my male."

My breath caught.

His male.

I was rendered speechless.

With a knowing smile, he pulled back the sheer curtain that concealed a darkened alcove. A long, earth-tone upholstered settee sat at the back next to a low table with chilled champagne and... a small pitcher of an oily substance that had me blushing momentarily. There was no one save us. A place for us and us alone, which was fine by me. Normally, I welcomed the company of others. I was a social butterfly after all, but with how incredible Myles looked this evening—wearing a button-down burgundy shirt that hugged every curve of his prominent chest—I decided I wanted to be here for him, just for him; his to look at while he'd be my male to ogle and touch.

As Myles poured us champagne from an awaiting bottle on a low table, I was filled with an inexplicable urge to move. He handed me my flute, and I downed the contents in one go, setting it aside as my focus remained fixed on him. I began dancing to the rhythm of the music that bled right into my very soul. As the melee of Fae and humans visible through the sheer curtain moved in sync—touching, feeling, living—my hips swayed from side to side, something that didn't escape his notice. His thorough examination of my half-unscaled body—a heady blend of hunger and heat—made my cock ache with unbearable need. I closed my eyes and let the music wash over me. Every tantalizing beat fueled my desire. The bass breathed life into my body, and when my chest tingled with awareness,

I felt him even before he'd carefully slotted his body against mine—his warmth enveloping me as he moved his hips. And, goddess. Could he *move*!

As he did this, my eyes remained closed, taking in all the sensations, and then something occurred to me.

I'd felt those moves before.

Under the guise of a mask.

I knew the movement of his body by heart because I'd committed every move to memory, so that I could savor it again and again and again. When Myles palmed my face and captured my lusty sigh within his mouth, the sensation of the moment overwhelmed me and nearly took me to my knees.

Myles just had to be my masquerade lover.

He had to be.

An inaudible whimper left my lips as he rolled his hips against me, like the roll of a wave melding to the shoreline, his tongue now tracing a line up my neck before he captured my earlobe between his teeth with a nip. "How I want to devour you. How I want to take you in every way possible."

"Please, take me," I breathed.

Who even was I?

"Now, now, my little minx. Let us savor the moment before I bring you to your pleasure."

The thought of waiting, the idea of not being able to bend over and let him sink his fat cock in my ass had me desperate with need. I wanted to feel all of him, *needed* to feel all of him, but Myles was determined to drag this out. With each passing song, his hands caressed up my thighs. With each thrumming beat, he drove his thick length against my backside. We remained in our little cocoon of lust and passion. A fire could ignite the curtain separating us from the rest of the revelry. That wouldn't stop the gathering crowd from casting curious, heated glances at us, just as they have now—our silhouettes clearly conspicuous. There was something sinfully erotic about being watched this way, barely visible like a clouded apparition. It only drove my need for Myles to breathless heights.

When he reached around my waist and slid his hand over my bulge, massaging and kneading, my legs wobbled and I leaned against his chest for support as he whispered, "You've been such a good boy, patiently waiting. And playing to our audience. How-ever shall I reward you?"

"Fuck me," I begged. "Please, fuck me."

He hummed against the skin of my neck. "Drop your scales, my pet."

I nearly whimpered like a faeling as my scales retreated, leaving me bare to all the realm. Myles peppered kisses down my spine—slowly, assuredly—until he came to sit on the low settee behind me, positioning his face level with my backside. I was exposed. Vulnerable.

His.

The tips of his fingers dug into my cheeks, parting them for his viewing pleasure. His thumb slowly pressed against my taut hole, probing. I bit my lip as he declared, "This is mine."

When his thumb left and was replaced by his tongue, a gasp left me, and my mouth parted on a moan as it swirled around the rim. "Oh my goddess." It was lewd and entirely unlike the image of Myles I'd been trying to hold onto—the refined side with polite words and acts of kindness that made my heart squeeze. This side of Myles had my heart squeezing for a set of different reasons. This side of Myles, I determined, would be mine and mine alone. This part of myself that let him kiss my most intimate parts in dark alcoves would be his. This was ours. My chest hummed in agreement.

As he pulled away, I longed for the feel of him until I felt something warm and slick on his fingers, spreading over my tiny hole with familiar skill. He gently lowered me to the crown of his girth, thick against my ass. I pushed back, rubbing against him lasciviously.

"Sit on my cock," he demanded in my ear.

With my hands met the clothe of his trousers hanging midway off his thighs, I glanced over my shoulder to witness the parting of his mouth as his stare fixed on where his cock pressed into me. "Fuck, yes," he grunted. The thick stretch was both new and familiar, and as I slid even further down, the way Myles gripped my hip, guiding me onto him, almost felt recognizable. "That's it, my pet. Take me. All of me."

And then, I pressed down on him entirely.

My head felt light, and I swam in a mental pool of desire so consuming that I nearly forgot where I was. If it hadn't been for the roll of Myles's hips against my ass, sinking him further into my channel while the sensual music encouraged our union, I'd have thought I was in a dream.

And then, Myles moved.

He became something wild, something *other*.

Something primal.

His fingers slid through my short hair in a tight grip and hauled my mouth to his while he fucked me with an intensity that stole my breath away. Thrust after thrust, I became his plaything, his to control.

And I let him.

"Surrender to me," he demanded against my lips, as if reading how my body responded to his. "Feel how I take you? Feel how I make you mine?"

"Yes."

"Good boy."

With a strength that robbed me of breath, Myles lifted us from the settee, holding me firmly against him with one arm caging me to his chest while his other hand gripped my hip to the point of pain. He fucked me. Hard. He hit that special spot with precision, as if he knew every fiber of my being, as if he were letting me know exactly who he was with the movement of his body. Myles was removing his mask with every intimate, crazed thrust. He and my masked lover were one and the same. I was sure of it. And as my seed shot from my cock, his hum of pure pleasure confirmed this.

"You fucking perfect, delicious creature. F—Fuck, Relio," he said in a filthy grunt of release.

Myles emptied himself within me, his cum filling me completely. Claiming me. I could feel his gaze travel over my shoulder to the crowd beyond the curtain, some with expressions of pure ecstasy and others openly pleasuring one another. All the while, their attention was firmly held in our direction.

We did that.

We did.

As he lowered us to the settee once again, his slow, open-mouthed kisses against my neck brought me down from the high he had given me. The way he held me in his own special way had me never wanting to leave the cradle of his arms again.

Myles Anthysius had unmasked me, body and soul.

And I was content to stay that way.

"Okay, I take back the comment about looking dicked down the last time I saw you."

I paused in my sketching and glanced at Tyla with a lifted brow. "And why is that?"

A smirk. "Because now you have the look of someone who's been properly dicked down, and the dark circles under your eyes to prove it."

I immediately padded the area in question. "Perhaps I was working hard last night."

"Oh, I bet you were working hard."

I dropped my pencil with a snap. "And what if I was?"

"Working *hard*?"

"Actually, my dear Tyla, it wasn't hard work at all." I paused, pursing my lips in thought, "Well, perhaps some of it was. That's the life of a bottom after all."

Surprise and delight lit Tyla's face, her mouth dropping open impossibly wide. "I knew it!"

"You knew nothing," I said as I continued to sketch, the corner of my mouth twitching.

Tyla leaned in conspiratorially. "Was it good?"

I couldn't help but return her glee. "It was beyond words."

"Well, you'd better try and find the words," she demanded, swatting my bicep. "I want all the details!"

And so, for the next half an hour, I spilled all the salacious details to Tyla, something I'd never do with anyone else but her. While I had many Fae and humans alike whom I called friends, I didn't trust that if I revealed these details to anyone other than Tyla, they'd be curious and want to taste the goods. My heart couldn't take betrayal like that. No, Tyla was the exception. She wouldn't do anything like that to me, and I wouldn't dare do anything like that to her. I suppose our friendship meant that much to one another.

"My, my. How things have progressed," she mused as she rested her chin on her palm with a blissful, knowing grin. "And here I thought this was just candlelit dinners, playful comments, and simmering glances."

My cheeks heated at the memory of last night. Myles and I went on—sensual dancing, kissing, fucking. It was a whirlwind of passion, desire, and something else I wasn't entirely ready to admit in front of my friend. "Myles has completely taken me by surprise," I admitted. "I didn't think he'd be capable of being so..."

"Dominant?" Tyla provided with a quirked brow.

"Yes. He's always so refined. And now? I have no doubt in my mind that he's my masked lover. The way he moved. The way he claimed me, and in front of everyone. I'd know those moves anywhere, Tyla. I've committed them to memory. It was as if he was letting me know exactly who he was with every move he made."

Tyla tapped her finger on the workshop table. "Does it change anything? Now that you know who your masked lover is?"

"Well," I began, twisting my head this way and that, "I can't exactly come out and ask him now, can I? That would make me look like a fool, especially if I'm wrong."

"Do you need him to confirm it?"

"I..."

The question gave me pause. Did I need him to confirm it? I absolutely knew in my soul it was him. And even so, in my heart, I was willing to admit that even if Myles wasn't my masked lover, the thought of waking up beside him with no masks and no fear held an appeal that made my chest ache. For once, the idea of commitment didn't scare me.

"No, I don't need him to confirm it, because truthfully, it wouldn't change how I feel about Myles. However, it *does* change how I feel about my masked male."

Her perfect dark hair shifted across her shoulders as she jerked back in surprise. "Wow. I wasn't expecting you to admit that." Her mouth widened in a bright smile. "I'm proud of you, you know?"

"Oh, stop," I said as I dashed a hand, turning my head to hide my blush. With a sigh, I glanced back at her. "Now what do I do?"

Tyla leaned across the worktable, placing a delicate hand on mine. "Now, you enjoy the life you deserve."

But a voice deep down inside me—some pestering, nagging voice within—whispered a warning that only I could hear, and

I couldn't help but wonder if the bottom was about to fall out from under me.

Chapter Eleven

P ERHAPS IT WAS OVERKILL to sketch so many designs for my queen, and maybe even more of an overkill to bring some of the designs to life—already cutting the patterns and stitching them in my workshop—without Queen Neleah advising which ones she preferred. But I wanted to ensure I was thoroughly prepared for the queen's review of her collection. In truth, I'd anticipated which designs would be to her liking. Some might call it foolish, but I prefer to call it intuitive. And if Francesca and Vebulah paid any attention to her style over the decades, they'd know she has a few tells: colors she tends to lean toward, lengths of dresses she seems to prefer. Being a good designer is about being observant and reading your client while also incorporating your own style, after all. And as I sat in the Queen's office, Myles standing stoically at her side as she reviewed what I'd created for her with a smile, I sat a little taller in my opulently upholstered chair.

"These truly are magnificent, Aurelio," she remarked, flipping to the next page and shaking her head. "How-ever will I choose?"

"It will be extraordinarily difficult, my queen," Myles told her, issuing me a wink she didn't see. "I do not envy you."

"Do not feel that you have to choose, Queen Neleah. I'm happy to create all the designs in the collection, if you so choose."

Her brow furrowed. "Are you certain? That is quite the un-dertaking."

"I'm certain. Winner or not, it would be my honor to bring the entire collection to life."

The queen's inquisitive perusal swept over me with approval. "You're absolutely as good as they say you are, huh?"

I leaned in with a snarky smirk. "Better."

The queen's laughter filled the room, and I couldn't help but imagine enjoying her company while working as the royal seamstress. She was so easy to like. Queen Neleah handed my sketchbook back to me. "I'd better leave you to it then. We'll see you in a few weeks' time, yes?"

I stood with a bow. "Yes, my queen. I'll have everything ready for your final fitting."

Glancing at Myles, my nerves settled as he gave me a calm, confident grin. "I'll see Mr. Martenos out," he told her.

The queen gave him a knowing smile. "Such a gentleman."

A beautiful scarlet heat bloomed on his cheeks as he placed his hand at the small of my back and escorted me out into the hallway. I stopped short at who was awaiting outside the office, although I should have expected it. "Vebulah."

"Aurelio." Her head snapped to Myles. "Secretary. How fortunate that you both are here. Together."

Some deep-seated dread sank to the bottom of my stomach, and the cold, calculating smirk on her face didn't help.

Myles stepped forward, towering over her, his posture alone making it clear. He would not be bullied today. "How may I help you, Miss Vella?"

Vebulah crossed her arms over her chest. "I thought I'd inform you that I saw the two of you at Pearl the other night."

Every hair on my body that wasn't beneath a scale stood on end, and I was quite certain that if I looked at myself in the mirror, my face would be drained of blood. This was my worst nightmare come to life. My absolute worst fear, and confirmation that the bottom had indeed fallen out from underneath me. Vebulah's satisfied demeanor did nothing but stoke the flames of my intuition.

Myles, however, remained cool, calm, and poised. "I'm not sure why our appearance at Pearl is of any matter to you."

"Of no matter to me?" She huffed in disapproval. "The two of you were seen by an entire floor of nobles and elites."

"We were in a private location," I implored.

"A sheer curtain blocking off an alcove does not serve as a private location, Aurelio. And since you all haven't publicly announced your relationship, I'd hazard a guess that the queen has no knowledge of your... relations. It's clear you were trying to keep this a secret." She narrowed her eyes on Myles. "Perhaps, Secretary, you wanted to use your power over Aurelio to garner sexual favors."

"He did no such thing," I defended, my ire rising.

Vebulah's head snapped to me, and judging by the evil smirk that grew, I realized I had walked right into her trap. "Oh? Then it would appear you seduced the poor Secretary for favor in the competition." She ignored my gasp and continued. "Either way, we'll have to see what the queen thinks about all of this."

Vebulah stepped forward to enter the office, but Myles blocked her way. "Please allow me to escort you inside, Miss Vella." He opened the door with a flourish and a glare that promised retribution, motioning her inside. Myles cast me a final look with something imploring winking in the shadows of his mahogany irises before he closed the door behind them, leaving me to stew in the dread and silence of the hallway. Despair slowly seeped into every part of my body. It grew like vines digging into my heart as I departed the palace for my workshop in a fog. I knew those vines would twist in a suffocating embrace.

And as the tears trailed down my cheeks, twist they did.

Tyla rubbed circles on my back while we sat on the couch in my living room, and I buried my face in my hands. "It's hopeless," I told her, my voice quivering as I tried and failed not to let my emotions peek through.

"It's not hopeless," she tried to reassure me.

I pulled my face away from the palms of my hands, and she winced. I'd been crying the entire afternoon. I had no doubt my eyes were as puffy as marshmallows.

I could really use a marshmallow right now.

Tyla reached for the chilled glass of white wine she'd poured for me and handed it over. "Here. Drink a little. It will settle your nerves."

"An entire bottle of Eliron Chardonnay couldn't calm my nerves right now. It's over, Tyla. Myles. My competition. Everything is over. The queen is going to think I seduced Myles for favor in the competition. I'm sure of it."

"You don't know that."

"Of course, I know that. What else is she supposed to think?" The deep sense of hopelessness settled at the very center of my being. "He's never introduced me as his partner. Maybe..." My bottom lip wobbled of its own accord. "Maybe he doesn't want me as his partner? Oh! I should have seen it from the start." I rubbed the tears out of my eyes. "How could I be so stupid?"

"Aury, he bought you every last flower... nay... every last rose in the queendom. Perhaps the lilies, too. He's been a gentleman, taking you out on proper dates, putting your needs first. I truly think you're overreacting here."

"I'm not overreacting."

Her unamused expression said otherwise.

"It's just…"—I let loose a pained sigh—"if I lose this competition, if I lose the opportunity to be the royal seamstress, my reputation in this city is ruined. And with my *esteemed* new owner, I'll be out of business and out on the street." I started to drag my hand through my hair before common sense prevailed, and I carefully placed the unruly strands back into place; I might have been upset, but that was no excuse for a messy hairstyle. "And then there's Myles. Things were going so well and—"

A knock on my apartment door, which sat above the shop, sounded, and I cast a curious glance at Tyla.

"I added him to your approvals list for access to the apartment," she informed me with a casual shrug.

My eyebrow arched to the sky. "And you didn't think to tell me?"

"I didn't think you'd mind." She stood from the couch and squeezed my shoulder. "I'll let him in and head out. Call me later, yeah? And remember, deep breaths."

I swallowed past the rising anxiety and closed my eyes. Whatever news Myles came with, however painful the news might be, I'd handle it as gracefully as I could. I blew out a long, steady breath, and when I opened my eyes, Myles stood before me with a grand look of concern, his hands resting in the pockets of his scaled trousers.

Ever the master in the art of deflection, I motioned around the room. "Welcome to my humble abode."

He spared a moment to take in the apartment, with its single room at the far end, a simple yet modern kitchen equipped with all the necessary amenities, and a quaint yet spacious living room. "It's lovely."

"I'm sure it's not as lovely as the royal seamstress's quarters in the palace, which I'll likely never see the inside of."

That sweeping gaze regarded me once again, making me feel infinitesimally small under his piercing stare, weighed down by apprehension. "Are you all right?" he asked, his tone like a warm balm that settled over my nerves.

I gave him a rueful smile. "I guess that all depends on the news you have from the palace."

Myles motioned to the couch. "May I?"

"Of course," I told him.

Myles slid onto the couch next to me and, with a comforting smile, said, "You're fine, darling."

I blinked a few times, thinking I might have misheard. "What do you mean, I'm fine?"

The corner of that smile began to twitch. "I mean, I took care of it for you."

"But... how?"

He reached up and placed a strand of hair that I had missed back in place with a reverence that made my heart swell. "We had to negotiate with Vebulah a bit, but in the end, she accepted finer fabrics in exchange for her silence and letting you stay in the competition."

A palpable relief settled over me, but it was short-lived when I realized Myles didn't share my sentiments—his expression carefully guarded. That's when it dawned on me. "It means we'll have to lay low, doesn't it?"

He reached out and grabbed my hand. "Just for a short time. Fashion Week is only a few short weeks away. It'll be here in no time."

Of course.

Of course, once I'd finally come to terms with the fact that I would submit to whatever this growing tension was in my heart and soul, something like this happened. And to have the queen involved? I shook my head. "I'm so very sorry if Queen Neleah sees you in a poor light now because of me."

Myles snorted uncharacteristically, and it captured my attention. "I do believe the queen was actually a little amused by all of this. I've seen her placate dignitaries far and wide with her deep nods of agreement and measured tone. Vebulah Vella was nothing compared to the other people she's had to deal with. The suggestion of finer fabrics from her"—Myles's fingers drew air quotes—"'secret' stores had Vebulah's eyes light up like a trident."

"I bet they did," I murmured, glancing away, knowing that I sounded like a petulant faeling.

His finger grazed the bottom of my chin, bringing my gaze back to his. "Does it really matter whether she has better fabrics or not?"

"No," I said with a sigh.

"That's correct. It doesn't, because you don't need better fabrics to win this competition, darling. You're going to do that with your talent and your talent alone. Your designs are magnificent. Miss Vella has to resort to such tactics because she doesn't hold a candle to you. It doesn't matter what we are to each other. She knows that, and the queen most certainly knows that. Otherwise, she would have let the accusations stand. Sometimes, we must let our competition think they have the upper hand. We must take the blows in silence. Our inner strength is our secret weapon. And wield it, we will; but until then"—at this, he leaned forward, bringing his lips within an inch of mine—"we'll slip our masks back on and hide our secret weapon where they will slowly forget about it until we strike. Yes?"

"Yes," I whispered.

"Good."

In the blink of an eye, he crashed his lips to mine—tongues tangled, passion fusing our every move. I wanted to meld myself to him, to truly make him mine. My need for this male would topple me from the cliff sides of Fortuna, where I was sure to meet my end.

But no. That's not right because Myles would always be there to catch me. And I wanted to show him just how much I appreciated that fact.

Like a priestess come to the temple to worship the goddess, I slid to the ground on my knees before him, his eyes widening in surprise. "What are you doing?"

I tapped a finger upon his bulge beneath his scales. "I'm taking care of my male."

There was a flicker of affection in his eyes, but it was quickly replaced by overpowering lust. Myles dropped his scales, freeing his glorious cock, and I licked my lips as it slapped on the prominent ridges of his abdomen with a delicious thump. I wasted no time taking that member within my hands, stroking a few times as I lifted myself, wrapping my mouth around his plump head with my eyes locked on him. I wanted to witness every ounce of pleasure on his face, and I did; his gasp was like a pin dropped in a silent room as I took his cock to the back of my throat and stayed there for a pause. I aimed to make him unravel with my tongue.

And I did.

I sucked Myles with conviction, my cheeks hollowing from the effort, and when his fingers slid into my hair, I hummed around him, his head dropping to the back of the couch with a moan that had my own cock begging to break free of its pocket.

"Goddess, Aurelio. That mouth is fucking divine. Oh!"

I took him all the way down my throat, and it flipped a switch in him. His fingertips dug into my skull as he began pumping into my mouth with abandon. Drool leaked from the corners of my lips, and my eyes watered with the effort to take his enormous girth—the stretch becoming too much and too little all at once.

With a loud plop, Myles pulled me off of him, breathing out of control, eyes wild with lust. "Stand."

I smirked. "Yes, sir."

His resounding groan left me deeply satisfied, and I stood, dropping my scales for his viewing pleasure. When he leaned forward and licked the precum off my jutting cock, I had to stifle my moan. He glanced up at me. "Lube?"

I pointed with a shaky finger at the basket on the side table. With a lifted brow, he reached inside, retrieving the tiny glass bottle.

I lifted a shoulder. "One must always be prepared."

He poured a generous amount into his palm, his fiery stare never leaving mine. "And you'll only be prepared for *me* moving forward."

"Is this your way of asking me to be exclusive?"

Guiding me to him with his free hand, Myles took his other and gently tipped the contents into the seam of my ass, and I whimpered like a needy little slut when he slipped his digits between my cheeks, massaging the tight hole. "You mistake me, darling."

"How so?" I breathed, his fingers probing me, going from gentle to demanding as he breached my entrance, pumping me slowly, tantalizingly.

"I wasn't asking." He pitched forward and licked my swollen head.

Shit.

"I was telling." In a sudden move that left me breathless, he spun me around. This dominant side of Myles had me wondering all sorts of things. It had me envisioning a world where I could have it all—the gentle Secretary who came to my rescue and the dominating male who could claim my body with a skill that had me desperate to submit. Pain radiated when his nails dug into the muscles of my backside, spreading me. "Now, sit on my cock while I watch this beautiful ass devour me whole."

With a cheeky glance over my shoulder, I slowly—ever so slowly—lowered myself, his mouth dropping open as his thick head breached my entrance. "Yes, that's it, darling. Mmm, fuck. You're so fucking tight."

Inch by delicious inch, he stretched me, and I couldn't hold back my moan when he shoved up and entered me completely. But moans turned to outright calls of ecstasy when I began gliding up and down his length, my thighs burning as I moved in time with his thrusts.

"You are so gorgeous like this, my pet. The warmth." His breath suddenly hitched. "So good."

A deep well of satisfaction bloomed, and I seized it, letting it fuel my confidence. I was his dirty little minx, and I would bring him his pleasure. My movements became frantic, my sacs slapping against his bare skin as I bounced on his dick, and when he swiveled his hips and hit that special spot within, the tingling sensation in my lower back grew. I was on the verge of coming all over the coffee table before me, all decency and decorum be damned.

But Myles Anthysius had other plans.

With his thick length still lodged within me, he lifted us from the couch and bent me over the coffee table, sending the glass of wine flying to the hardwood floor and breaking into a million tiny pieces.

"Grip the edge, darling," he ordered huskily.

And as I did, Myles's control snapped.

Hips pushing into me with brutal need, he fucked my tight hole and I called out with heady pleasure—all capable thought leaving me, replaced with the feel of Myles working me with a skill only he could execute. The low coffee table scraped across the floor with each slap of his hips against my backside. My need was evident in my cry of pleasure when his hand came to my neck, pinning me to the surface while he reached around my hip and began stroking my cock—his palm still slick with oil and gliding across my rock-hard length with ease. "Myles!"

"Yes, my pet. That feels good, doesn't it? Mmmm. Fuck. You look stunning when you're about to come, and I know you want to come for me. So, come for me."

I needed no more instruction. With a few skilled strokes of his hand and a few hard thrusts, I came at his mercy, spilling within his palm.

"That's it. Fuck. I'm—"

His cock began pumping in my channel, and I arched my back to meet his final thrust, reaching so far in me, I thought he'd never come out.

Hot.

Warm.

Safe.

Myles was all those things. And mine.

Sensing that I wasn't quite ready for him to leave my body, he carefully guided us back to the couch, pulling my back into his chest, peppering soft kisses across my neck, my ear, inhaling deeply when our heads rested side by side on the pillow. I'd never felt so treasured, so cherished in all my life.

Eventually, he pulled out of me and summoned water, tending to every last inch of my body with tenderness as I lay languid and motionless in the warmth of his arms. As sleep consumed me, a vision of Myles and me in his palace quarters drifted in my mind—lying side by side on a soft mattress with nothing but mountains of pillows for company, a beautiful life with my bondmate, one that allowed me to sleep soundly throughout the night.

Chapter Twelve

THE NEXT DAY, THE warm Atlantian sunrays streamed through the floor-to-ceiling windows of the shop, adding to my already bright mood. I'd been smiling since the moment I woke up, remembering the previous night and how my lover handled me—cared for me.

Loved me, perhaps?

But no—it was too early to think of love. Of course, if Myles were truly my bondmate, then love would be too weak a word for what we had together, and didn't that just widen my smile? My thoughts were still fixed on Myles as I straightened a wayward sleeve on a rack, and the shop bell chimed. "Welcome to Enchanted Couture," I called without looking.

"Doesn't seem very enchanting at all."

I froze, all the happiness leaving my body in a millisecond. I slowly turned to meet the owner of that high-pitched, nasally voice.

Melysah Velafyn, head of the Atlantian Council and owner of Behuko Enterprises, stood at the front of the shop, glaring at my garments as if they'd offended her very being. When she turned to me, her scowl was little more than a greeting. "Do people actually buy these clothes?"

Did I mention how much I can't stand her?

I backed away from the rack and approached her with all the sway in my hips I could muster, letting my critical gaze roam over the lackluster clothing she'd worn today.

Vebulah Vella's clothing, I noted.

"Since you're clearly not here to shop, is there something I can help you with?"

A chill ran down my spine when a saccharine smile spread on her pale face. "Actually, there is." She clasped her hands at her middle. "You will drop out of the competition."

All the air left my lungs. "Excuse me?"

"Are you hard of hearing?" She fucking tsked, raising her voice. "You will drop out of the competition," she said slowly.

"I heard you the first time, you pathetic little bitch."

"Watch it, Mr. Martenos," she warned, ire crawling into her eyes. "That is no way to speak to the owner of your building."

Unchecked fury—unlike any I'd felt before—hovered on the tip of my tongue.

"You should never have been allowed to compete in the first place. Your designs are nothing compared to Vebulah's. Mediocre at best. Now, you will be dropping out of the contest. Effective today."

"I most certainly will not."

"You will. Otherwise, you'll be evicted from this building effective tomorrow, without a store or a home to call your own."

The retort swept out of me as I realized the absolute power she wielded over me. She wanted me out of the competition. The question was: "Why?"

Melysah tipped her chin up. "Not that I owe someone such as yourself an explanation, but I'll give it to you nonetheless." A darkness crept into her features. "I tire of Queen Neleah and her silly little antics, such as this contest. It's beneath her station. She brings shame to the throne of Atlantis."

"You sound a little jealous there, Councilor. Such traitorous thoughts."

The casual tilt of her head sent a sliver of fear down my spine, and I couldn't help but wonder about her deeper motivations—whether she aimed to get back at a queen she despised for no good reason, or if she sought something bigger, something at odds with the Elemental Mark on her wrist, which did *not* belong to a queen. I was not ignorant of the whispers across Atlantis from the rebel group, the Akani, who believed humans were beneath them and that a new queen would rise to aid their cause. One had to wonder *who* that queen might be.

"I speak only of this stupid challenge," she pivoted with her words. "What a waste of time it is to contend for the position of Royal Seamstress when there's only one designer fit for the position."

"Let me guess. Vebulah Vella."

"See, even you know she's better than you." She dragged her gaze over me with a disgust I hadn't witnessed in an age. "I cannot understand what he sees in you. Borike'n gutter filth such as yourself doesn't belong anywhere near a refined and esteemed male like Myles Anthysius. But I suppose even gentlemales need something to use to scratch their itches."

I could feel the tears threatening to spill forth, and I swallowed past that urge. I wouldn't let this female witness my emotions.

"Plus," she stepped forward, her thin lips flattening in a firm line, "I don't particularly like you, if I'm being honest. And I always put those who belong beneath the weight of my feet in their place."

There was no holding my tongue then. My hurt morphed into righteous rage. "I belong under no one's shoes, least of all yours, since they were likely bought at some bland establishment that matches the rest of your wardrobe. Now, you've made your request. I believe there's nothing more for you to say."

"I could go on, but I have more important matters to tend to." She lengthened her spine. "Your withdrawal?"

"Yes," I said through gritted teeth. "I will send word to the palace of my withdrawal from the competition."

Melysah smiled supremely. "Excellent. A wise choice."

"Now get the fuck out of my shop."

She pursed her thin lips to the side in thought. "Technically, it's my shop."

"And I'm your tenant with rights of my own. Please leave."

"Very well," she said with a dramatic sigh. "Either way, I got what I wanted." With a final disgusted glance at my garments, she turned and departed. The vision of her strolling down the block became blurred not a moment later.

"You can't be serious."

Tyla sat across the high-top table at Tridentinis with an expression that was a blend of surprise and anger as I swirled my tooth-picked olive around the rim of my martini glass. "As serious as a shoe sale at Slay's."

"Fuck."

"Yup."

"Betty!" Tyla called to the bartender, who glanced up from the bar top she'd been cleaning. "Another round, please."

"Coming right up!" Betty called.

Tyla sank into her seat with a pained sigh. "Is there really nothing that can be done?"

"It's already done," I told her, my tone mournful even to my own ears. "I've sent the message to the queen thanking her for letting a gutter rat such as myself enter the competition in the first place."

Tyla tsked. "You didn't say that."

"No, I didn't, but I might as well have." I downed the rest of my martini, wincing as Betty placed another on the table. "I just thanked her for the opportunity and informed her that I'm withdrawing from the competition."

"And have you informed Myles of this?"

"No, not yet," I said, biting the olive off my toothpick and plunking it into the empty glass Betty held out for me. She turned toward the bar as the juices trickled down my throat and were just as bitter as my mood. "There's nothing he can do anyway. He can't force Melysah to keep me in the building. She has the upper hand. And..."

I paused for a beat, not believing what I was about to admit. Tyla dipped into my line of vision, which had drifted to the table. "And?"

I inhaled deeply. "And Myles is worth backing out of the competition for. Myles is worth keeping my business for. I may never be the Royal Seamstress, but hopefully—if he's ready to claim me as his—I can be his bondmate, and that's worth far more than any position in the palace. Even the queen's position."

The corner of Tyla's mouth twitched. "You'd make a magnificent queen, though."

"I would, wouldn't I?"

Tyla straightened. "Well, fuck that competition. You ended up winning the best prize of all." She raised her glass. "To claiming Prince Charming."

"To claiming Prince Charming," I echoed, clanking my glass against hers.

"Mr. Martenos?"

I swiveled around in my chair and found the palace messenger staring back at me, my brow furrowing. "Yes?"

He handed me a sealed envelope, the queen's crest imprinted in the ruby red wax. "For you."

"But... how did you know how to find me?"

He winced with a smile. "The Secretary said that if you weren't at the shop, I'd likely find you here."

"Prince Charming strikes again," I heard Tyla murmur.

With a formal bow, the messenger left me in bewilderment.

"Well, don't sit there," Tyla admonished with a dart of her delicate hand. "Open it."

I did, ripping open the envelope and scanning the beautiful cursive script on the page. I gasped when I reread it.

"What does it say?" Tyla asked.

My wide eyes swung to her. "I've been summoned to the palace tomorrow morning for an audience with the queen."

Chapter Thirteen

MY NERVES HUMMED LIKE bees in a hive as I trailed behind the palace escort. The walls of the darkened hallway felt as though they might cave in on me with each step. I didn't know what conversation awaited me on the other side of the queen's office door, but with the escort's deafening knock echoing in the barren hallway, I was about to find out.

"Come in," came the queen's muffled voice from the other side. When the escort opened the door, I drew a breath and stepped across the threshold.

And paused.

Queen Neleah sat at her desk with steepled hands, her blue-eyed stare reflecting her authority in every way. And then, there was Myles, standing tall and proud at her side—his face revealing nothing as his attention hooked on mine.

"Take a seat, Mr. Martenos," Queen Neleah ordered.

My legs shook as I made my way across the room and lowered myself into the plush chair before her desk after a brief curtsy. "My queen," I began, not knowing what else to say.

Her long sigh took me aback. "I received your letter informing me of your withdrawal from the competition."

"Oh. That."

"Yes. That," she echoed. "Care to explain?"

I chanced a glance at Myles, whose eyebrow moved into a perfect arch. Clearing my throat, I said, "You see, your Majesty, I've had some time to reflect, and I... uh... well"—I cleared my throat again—"the last thing I would want is for my relationship with Myles to be seen as the reason I'd win the competition."

"But we've already established that Vebulah would receive the finer fabrics in exchange for her silence."

I didn't have the heart to inform her that Vebulah had already opened her big, fat mouth to Melysah, so I went in a different direction. "We had established that, Your Majesty. But... Myles means more to me than any competition, and I've decided to choose him." When my gaze traveled to Myles once more, his expression softened.

"Well, if that isn't the most romantic thing I've heard in ages, then I don't know what is," Queen Neleah remarked. "But, declarations of love aside, I do not see the conflict of interest. At the end of the day, *I'm* the one who decides the winning designer, not Myles. Quite frankly, I couldn't care less if the two of you dated or fucked in an orgy in front of everyone at Temple Park. Your relationship doesn't matter one way or another. So, you have no reason to drop out of the competition."

Shit.

Shit. Shit. Shit.

The victorious curl of her lips told me there was no escaping this. But I couldn't compete. I stood to lose everything. It left me with only one choice.

The truth, the whole truth, and nothing but the truth, so help me goddess.

On the tail end of a heavy exhale, I confessed, "Councilor Velafyn threatened to kick me out of my shop—and my home—if I didn't drop out of the competition."

Myles gasped, his mouth opening in shock.

But it was Queen Neleah's face that fell into one of pure, palpable anger, sending a shiver down my spine. "She *what*?"

"She's the owner of Behuko Enterprises and just recently acquired my building," I told her. "She threatened my very livelihood, my queen. And in the event that I lose this competition—because while I'm confident, I wouldn't dare to be presumptuous—I'd stand to lose my business, for which I worked very hard, as well as my apartment above the shop." My bottom lip trembled as I regarded Myles. "Besides, I meant what I said. While the competition means everything to me, so does Myles."

Queen Neleah recaptured my attention with a glare that could have cut ice. "I'd bet my bottom dollar that's why Francesca Bonaflyn pulled out of the competition as well."

Well, that was news.

"She owns most of the Fashion District now, my queen," I informed her. "I wouldn't doubt she threatened Francesca as well."

"Goddess, how I despise that female," she seethed. "What she seeks to gain from this is beyond me."

"Aside from the satisfaction of undermining you?" At this, the queen dashed a hand in the air as if Melysah's efforts were nothing more than a gnat. "I do believe she's a fan of Miss Vella's designs."

The queen snorted.

Snorted.

"Miss Vella is only in the competition because I recognized your designs in her shop. I wanted to expose her for the fraud that she is." My mouth fell open as a cheeky smirk appeared on the queen's face. "Don't look so surprised. I relish in the drama."

My mouth snapped shut. "Noted."

"As for your place in the competition, as well as Miss Bonaflyn's," she continued, "you'll both show your designs during Fashion Week, Melysah be damned. Don't worry about her. I'll take care of it."

I swallowed past the rising emotions. "Thank you so much, Your Majesty," I whispered.

"Myles?"

"Yes, my queen," he replied, ever the Secretary ready to do her bidding.

"The gardens are lovely this time of year. Perhaps you and Mr. Martenos would care for a stroll? There's a charming gazebo by the Shingu River. The two of you won't be bothered. I'll see to it."

A scarlet flush bloomed on Myles's cheeks. "Thank you for your generosity, my queen. That would be wonderful."

"When you return, summon Miss Bonaflyn to the palace again. And swing by Roarvyn's office on the way to the gardens, would you? Let him know to meet me here immediately. I believe there are explicit rules regarding property ownership while serving on the Council. As the Council's expert, he'll know exactly where to look."

"As you wish, Your Majesty," he said with a bow. Myles held out his hand to me, his features so incredibly striking and handsome when he smiled the way he did. I melted for him all over again. "Shall we?" he asked.

Placing my hand in his, my cheeks suddenly flushed hot. "We shall." He drew me into his side as we made for the door.

"And Aurelio?" the queen called.

I glanced over my shoulder with Myles's hand still in mine. "Yes, Your Majesty?"

"I expect you to blow away the competition," she said with a grin. "That's a direct order from your queen."

Elation. Pure elation roared through me. "You got it, my queen."

Sunrays shimmered like thousands of sparkling diamonds across the surface of the Shingu. We strolled through the garden in companionable silence as we passed by fat, blooming roses of every color, and trickling waterfalls that led into shallow ponds filled with koi fish the size of tabby cats. My hand remained in his the whole time, and every sneaked glance held a deeper meaning; every knowing smile carried with it the declaration I'd made in the queen's office.

When we arrived at a charming gazebo that sat in front of the river, it seemed as if Myles couldn't hold back his sentiments any longer. He cupped my face and brought his lips to mine, kissing me softly, slowly—as if we had all the time in the world and no place to be. My heart immediately sped in my chest as I snaked my hands around his waist. As he drew away, searching my face as if I were the most precious thing in his world, it stirred something so profoundly deep in my chest.

Something that *hummed*.

"My dearest Aurelio," he said above a whisper. "Your confession in Queen Neleah's office has given me hope that you are ready to remove the masks we've worn for far too long."

I brushed my nose against his. "Are we talking about metaphorical masks? Or the real ones we've worn at the Starlit Masquerade?"

His perfect smile—all bright, white teeth and gleaming—spread on his handsome face. "I have waited a long time to answer that question. In this case, the answer is both the metaphorical masks and the ones we've worn at our ball, meeting in secret decade after decade." He pressed his mouth to my jaw and whispered, "Yes, I am your masked lover."

"I fucking knew it," I said, slapping his bottom playfully.

"But I'm not done confessing."

"You're not?" I asked with a quirked brow.

"No, my darling. I am not." Another chaste kiss. "There are so many wonderful things I adore about you: how outspoken you can be, crass at times, incredibly catty."

"Some might say those things get me in trouble."

He chuckled. "That is true, but it's one of the many things I love about you."

My breath halted.

"But what I *truly* love about you is how you have a heart of gold, and your loyalty, when given, goes beyond friendship. It's ironclad. You genuinely care for those around you, and it shows to anyone who cares to notice."

I blinked away the tears that welled in my eyes, his thumb not missing a beat as he brushed them away. I shook my head. "Many might wonder why someone with such incredible etiquette, who's calm and well-spoken, would want to be with a Borike'n gutter rat like me."

He jerked back, a crease forming on his brow. "A gutter rat?"

"Melysah's words, not mine."

Anger lit like a blowtorch in his expression. "You are not to listen to a word that female says. Understood? Not about you, and certainly not about me. For the first time in my life, I feel that I can embrace who I genuinely am. It is such a privilege to reveal all the parts of myself to someone I trust and love beyond measure, to share the parts of me that no one but you will ever get to see. No one but you." His hands were gliding down my neck, my arms. "I get to indulge in all of my deepest, darkest fantasies with you. The mask of propriety I wear in front of everyone else is the true mask I wear. But you?"

His hands smoothed over the curves of my backside, spreading goosebumps across my skin, both above and beneath my scales. "The male I've fallen in love with, the male who has my whole body, my whole soul. You get all of me. You are the one I plan to present before the goddess as my bondmate. You and no one else."

"Truly?" I asked, my voice wavering.

"Truly. I love you, Aurelio Martenos. Please let me present you? Let us solidify this bond so that we may share an eternity of dances together at the Starlit Masquerade. Say yes."

A tidal wave of tears emerged in my eyes. It was only a short time ago that I scoffed at the notion of bondmates. Never in a millennium did I think the goddess had deemed me worthy of a mate, but here was this wonderful male—strong, sexy as fuck, intelligent, and dashing.

And he was just for me.

Mine.

"Yes," I whispered.

A look of relief crested across his striking features. "Thank the goddess."

Myles captured my cry in a passionate, all-consuming kiss that would have brought me to my knees had it not been for his grip digging into my thighs and pulling me into him. He slammed me up against the gazebo post, and it creaked ever so slightly as he pressed me up into it. Then his hands moved everywhere, sliding up my back, kneading and smoothing my muscles, threading through my hair, all the while his tongue skillfully danced with mine. A moan left me, and he captured that too. This patient, beautiful soul—who'd waited nearly an eternity for me to be ready to move beyond the masks we wore—molded to my body like he belonged there.

Because he did.

He absolutely did.

And goddess, when his hips swiveled repeatedly into mine, I thought I might perish on the spot. His rock-hard length rubbed against my cockpocket, and I desperately wanted to feel the skin of his dick against my own.

"Drop them," he ordered, as if reading my mind. "Drop them now."

"But someone might—"

"I couldn't give a fuck if they did. Drop your scales, my mate."

Without further ado, I dropped my scales, and a whimper left my lips when his scaled bulge pushed into the muscles of my abdomen, my raging length. Still scaled just below his hips, Myles's prominent chest—with all its dips and crevices—was on full display for my viewing pleasure and I took a moment to drink him in.

"Goddess. I'll never tire of you looking at me like that," he breathed. "Reach into my pocket."

With a salacious grin, I reached between his legs, the scales parting for me as I breached his cockpocket and was met by the smooth skin of his engorged erection—my grin widening when he hissed.

"Not that pocket, darling."

"Oh, no?" I asked innocently, stroking him.

"No, but feel free to continue while you reach into the scaled pocket of my trousers."

"My pleasure." My hand moved up and down his length as I reached into the pocket at his thick, muscular thigh and huffed a laugh at what I found inside. I pulled out the tiny bottle of lube.

When I cast him a questioning look, a salacious grin curved soft and slow. "One must always be prepared."

I leaned forward, "And you'll only be prepared for me moving forward?"

His hands came up to cup my face, adoration swimming under his beautiful lashes. "I'll only be prepared for you *forever*." Our mouths molded together as the drop of his scales tickled my abdomen, leaving him gloriously nude before me. "Now, reach down and get my dick nice and slick. I want to make love to my mate."

The lube was cool in my palm as I lathered Myles's girth from tip to base. He watched me with heated intensity as I did, leaving me incredibly restless for him to take me. Command me. When he motioned for the bottle and began pouring the contents into the crack of my ass, my heart skipped with anticipation. His long, elegant fingers spread the substance around my tight hole, breaching it a time or two to ensure I was ready.

And I was more than ready.

I wanted Myles Anthysius with an unparalleled fierceness that could topple mountains.

My Myles.

My mate.

With a strength that left me breathless, Myles gripped my thighs, hoisting me up against the gazebo post, and with one arm holding me up, he knocked the head of his swollen cock to my entrance. His eyes never left mine as he slowly slid into me, my tiny pants mingling with his warm exhales, mirroring the effort it took him not to slide home too fast. As he entered another inch, a whimper left me. He was so impossibly big. I felt he might split me.

"That's it, my pet," he breathed raggedly, pushing my thighs apart to gain purchase. "I wish you could see how stunning you are, taking my cock like a good boy." He slammed the rest of the way in.

"Fuck!"

"Yes. Let's."

Myles pumped in and out of me with a precision that left me wanton and needy. I captured his mouth, my tongue twirling with his as he fucked me with abandon. I was his pet to keep, his male to use as he pleased. And goddess, how I loved that. I *really* fucking loved that.

His grunt of pure pleasure had me hardening to painful levels. My release was threatening, and a trail of pre-cum trickled down my cock.

"Stroke yourself," he ordered between measured, frantic thrusts. "I want you to come all over me. Mark me. Make me yours, my mate."

That mouth.

That dirty fucking mouth.

"Whatever you desire, my love."

"Goddess!" he grunted.

I made swift work of stroking my length, my need causing my lower back to tingle unbearably. Myles watched my movements with rapt attention until, finally—*finally*—I came with a fury unlike any other. Cum spilled forth and landed on the plains of his tight abdomen. My mouth fell open in ecstasy as Myles moaned his pleasure, giving one, two, and a third a final fierce thrust in my channel—his thick girth pumping his seed deep within me. My head swam with lust and fatigue as we came down from the high. My head came to rest on his shoulder, burying my face in the crook of his neck to steady my breathing. Suddenly, Myles wrapped my legs around his waist and carried me out of the gazebo, both of us stark naked as the day we were born.

"Where are we going?" I asked in amusement.

Myles brushed a kiss to my cheek. "I'm going to clean my mate in the Shingu."

With determined strides, the water splashed around Myles's ankles as we entered the shallow river—the cool, refreshing water rising to our waists. And yet, he still held me in his arms, still looking at me in that way of his that made my chest tingle all over. A slow smirk emerged on his face. "You feel it too, don't you?"

I glanced away, unable to look at him, but Myles remained determined. Placing his fingers on the tip of my chin, he guided my focus back to him. "You don't have to be afraid." A denial sat on the tip of my tongue, but one look at his arched brow kept me silent. "I am yours. You are mine. And the future is ours—ours to share together, ours to experience as one. You never have to worry about me leaving you. I haven't been able to for all these long decades. Even the small scrap of existence in your life as your masked lover each year was necessary for me.

I shook my head in disbelief. "You should have said something."

He cast me a rueful smile. "And you think you would have been ready for all of this?"

I had to think on it. Really think. Because the days of denial—about bondmates being bullshit and commitment being an outrageous idea—just ended a few weeks ago when I was able to wholly embrace what I was feeling for Myles. "No, I wouldn't have been ready."

"And it's perfectly acceptable that you weren't," he assured me. "The goddess might have made us for each other, but her timing is always perfect. This is our time. This is our moment. And..." Myles shook his head.

"And what?" I asked.

"How lucky I am to be destined to walk with you in this life." He cupped my face. "And now, I get to watch you as you rise above your competition and claim the role you have always been destined for. I'm honored to be by your side to witness it."

There were no further words. I couldn't possibly ruin the moment with a cheeky remark or a self-deprecating comment. So rather than do any of that, I brought my lips within an inch of his and whispered, "I love you, Myles. Let us claim our future together."

And sealed our destiny with a kiss.

Chapter Fourteen

"Not that one, Tyla."

"You just said to steam this one."

"I most definitely did not. I said the royal blue garment."

"This is the royal blue garment."

"The other royal blue garment!"

"You have to be more specific!"

This had been how the afternoon unfolded—filled with anxiety, panic, and a deep longing for a strong martini. Not that I would indulge in such a thing just hours before my debut, before the entire city of Atlantis descended on Fashion Week.

Not before the biggest moment of my life. "Oh, this is going to be a disaster."

Tyla peeked at me from behind the royal blue garment—the correct one this time. "Would you stop with the dramatics, Aury? You're going to have a nervous breakdown, and the full hour you spent styling your outfit and hair will have been completely wasted."

I gasped. "Don't fling such bad juju into the cosmos!"

"Well, then. Take a deep breath and get your shit together, bestie. You have a competition to win," she encouraged with a wink.

Deep breaths.

Yes.

I could do that.

Breathe.

Just then, the front door chime sounded. I nearly opened my mouth to tell them to go away—something that could seriously cripple my customer service vibes in the city—when I noticed the palace messenger with an envelope in hand.

"Mr. Martenos?"

Fuck. This can't be good. "That's me."

Face incredibly impassive, he handed me the note and, not a moment later, was out the door. Panic stitched its way through my gut like a fiercely pointed needle and came out the other side. I flipped over the envelope and beheld the seal on the ruby-red wax.

The seal that was most definitely *not* the royal crest.

But the Anthysius crest.

A smile instantly spread across my face as I ripped open the envelope with renewed energy, but when I scanned the contents inside, I felt the blood drain from my face.

"What is it?" Tyla asked, coming beside me.

"I..."

I couldn't speak. I could barely even breathe.

Tyla snatched the letter from my grasp and read each word for herself. Her eyes widened, and jumped up to me. "Holy shit. Aurelio—"

"I know. Blessed Goddess above." My chest pumped with the effort of drawing air into my lungs.

Because the letter in Tyla's hand was no letter, it was a formal deed of transfer for my shop from Behuko Enterprises to...

Me.

And the second piece of parchment, in simple script—a script that likely had been practiced over centuries for how elegant it was—read:

Yours. Always.

Heart thumping wildly, I peered around the midnight black curtain, and my mouth dropped open at the sheer number of Atlantians gathering around the catwalk slicing through the middle of Temple Park. I let loose a sound somewhere between a whimper and a groan. There were so many people. Too many people. A tingly feeling spread all over my face and neck.

Suddenly, the curtain pulled taut, blocking my view. Tyla's scolding glare met mine as I glanced to the side. "You're not supposed to look."

"How can you expect me not to look?"

Pulling me around by the shoulder, she said, "I expect you to be there for your models."

"But Tyla—"

"No 'buts,' Aury. You're going to give yourself a heart attack."

My brow furrowed. "But Fae can't really get heart attacks."

She rolled her beautiful, almond-shaped eyes. "You'd likely be the first. Now, come on."

We sashayed through a backstage crowd of models and make-up artists, as well as a few nobles seeking to appear important by mingling with the other designers and their entourages. The slow, steady bass accompanied our steps as we passed Vebulah's area. Even as her models were striding down the runway, I could feel her glare on me.

Good.

Let her look her fill at the winner.

I wouldn't give her a second of my time.

Squaring my shoulders, determination coursing through me as I clapped my hands, addressing my team, "All right, queens and flame dames. We're about to begin. Does anyone need any last-minute adjustments?"

Wrong question to ask.

The group erupted in a flurry of final requests. Tyla and I immediately sprang into action—a nip of the string here and an adjustment of the fabric there. Before we knew it, my name was being called through the hum of activity.

"Mr. Martenos! You're up in five!"

"Fuck."

"Breathe," Tyla ordered from where she crouched, sewing a loose hem on a model. She rose, giving her work one last inspection. "Okay, we're ready."

I blew out a long breath and closed my eyes, reining in all the emotions swirling in my gut.

"Mr. Martenos!"

"I know! Five minutes!"

The stagehand shook his head as he approached. "That's not it. Here." He shoved a piece of parchment in my hand and left just as quickly. With my brows dipping, I ripped open the parchment, and my fear instantly morphed into elation.

Darling,

You're going to do amazing. Remember that no matter what, we've already won.

Yours,

Myles

I exhaled all the bullshit I'd been feeling before I read his letter and let those words sink in. He was right, of course. I had already won because, no matter what, I had the safety of my shop, which I now owned—something he and I would talk about later—and I had... him. It was a strange sensation, knowing that my life was fulfilled in a way I'd never dreamt of before.

"Tyla!"

"Yes, Aury," she sing-songed a few paces away.

I cast her look brimming with confidence, and a smile lit her lovely face.

"Let's do this."

The half hour was a blur of memories. Anxiety. The thrill. The vibes. The boom of the bass coursed through my body as I watched the show unfold. I felt like I was sailing through it. Every model hit their steps with surgical precision. Every fabric flowed around their bodies exactly as designed, hugging every luscious curve and complementing their beauty. All the while, I stood backstage beyond the catwalk, arms folded as the corners of my lips occasionally twitched with a smile I couldn't possibly contain. By the time the final model—the absolute showstopper—strolled down the runway, I was a ball of emotions, both happy and relieved. I watched with rapt attention as my model, wearing the very same mask Myles affixed to my bouquet, drew the crowd in. Her gown swam between violet and purple in the faelights, with the emblem of a bondmate mark stitched over the fabric of her left breast.

It was then that I felt the sensation of being watched. I scoured the crowd until I found the one pair of mahogany eyes—eyes that, unlike the rest of the crowd, were firmly fixed on me. A wicked smile slowly spread across his handsome features. He knew; he absolutely knew. This last design was an homage to him and everything we shared both behind the mask and without it. It signified our past, our present, and our future. And when the queen leaned into Myles's side, whispering into his ear with a smile of pure delight, I had no doubt in my mind that this fashion competition was mine to win.

So, when the queen stepped onto the stage and greeted the crowd with a flourish of her own—with a pause for the dramatics—I could only bury my face in my hands as Aurelio Martenos fell from her lips and boomed across the park. My team enveloped me in a group hug filled with jumping, screaming, and excitement. I could barely draw any breath into my lungs.

"You did it!" Tyla screamed. "You're the next Royal Seamstress!"

"Our social life just took a major step!" I teased.

She gripped me tightly in a hug, and when she pulled away, her attention drifted over my shoulder. The smirk was telling enough. I turned.

And there he was.

My Myles.

My mate.

And I was pleased to find that he chose one of my designs for the occasion—a pitch black suit that hugged every curve of muscle from his broad shoulders down to his shiny shoes. Needing no invitation, Myles slid his arms around me with a smile. "I told you so."

I huffed a light laugh. "So you did."

"Congratulations," he whispered against my lips until he kissed me soundly in front of everyone. My team's catcalls had me laughing into his kiss. As I pulled away, I recalled the bone I had to pick with him. "You bought me a building," I said, and it was not a question.

He placed a strand of hair back in place. "I made an investment."

"In my name."

"Whose name it's in hardly matters."

I smoothed a finger over the fabric of his chest. "Did you think I was going to lose?"

He jerked back, puzzled. "No. I just didn't want you to feel like you didn't have a choice. You may have won the competition, but I wanted you to feel like you always had something to call your own." A shrug. "Just in case the palace life doesn't suit you."

With a feline smile, I wrapped my arms around his neck. "Oh, palace life will suit me just fine."

"I'm sure it will." He searched my face then, part longing and part admiration. "I love you, Aurelio. I'm so proud of you, and I can't wait to witness our future together."

My heart bloomed with joy. "And I love you."

There, under the canopy of faelights and branches, I kissed my mate, knowing that whatever the future held, I was right where I belonged.

By his side.

Epilogue

Myles

O BSESSED.

I was utterly obsessed with Aurelio Martenos Anthysius—my newly bonded mate. My heart swelled at the thought.

I could tell you that this obsession of mine was one born purely out of lust and need alone, but I'd be lying to you if I did. I've been told that I am a patient male. Patience might as well have been my middle name. I'd had plenty of practice with waiting. But at the end of the day, I knew the reward would be oh so satisfying.

Aurelio was worth the agony of knowing what he was to me, yet still being unable to complete the bond. So I was patient. I played the game year after year, decade after decade. Per the rules, there were no names, no significant ways to identify each other. So I'd donned my black mask, adorned with glimmering diamonds in filigree swirls, so that my lover would recognize me. Now, the bond humming between us had stripped away our anonymity. The pull I felt toward him was telling enough.

Take, for example, what I'm feeling right now as I cut a pathway through the crowded ballroom floor of the Starlit Desires Masquerade.

I could feel him.

Like a phantom caress enticing my very soul.

My Aurelio.

Goddess, my cock stirred just remembering our trysts—his alluring face, skin so soft it might have been carved from the smoothest marble. My fingers tingled as shiny strands of his dark hair—hair I planned to take within my grasp in just a few moments—danced in my mind's eye. The thought of plunging into his magnificent ass invigorated me.

And then, I saw him. Standing in the center of the dance floor, bare from the waist up, wearing nothing but his deep red mask and matching trousers, bejeweled with the same intricate designs. It had my manhood positively weeping.

The low glow emanating from the string lights above his head bathed him in a warmth that highlighted the mask that ran along the lines of his cheekbones and jaw, setting his mesmerizing amber eyes alight with a sparkle. A cool breeze whipped through the open-air courtyard, but his dark hair remained intact—not a strand out of place. When I reached him, my attention lingered over the lines of his sculpted shoulders, down the perfect frame of his chest, to the perfectly tailored trousers that hugged his lean thighs. He was stunning. Absolutely stunning. A part of me felt unworthy to be his. But I must have done something right, because the goddess seemed fit to bless me with him.

"You take my breath away, darling," I said, my desire for him dripping in my tone despite my best effort.

With a slow sway of his delectable hips, Aurelio closed the distance between us with a devilish smirk. "Tonight, I'm not your darling." He pressed his soft lips to mine, once. Twice. "Tonight, I'm the servant at your mercy, and you are the master of my body."

Fuck. Me.

I let loose a groan. "Damn you and that mouth. It will be the death of me."

His tongue traced a path along the seam of my lips. "Funny. I thought my mouth could bring you to life."

"That it will." My mouth crashed into his instinctively in a way that was both parts ravenous and possessive.

Just the way I liked it.

I pulled away, breathless. "Meet me upstairs in our usual location. I want you undressed, save for your mask, and on your knees."

A flash of teeth greeted me as he grinned. "Yes, sir," he complied, the glint of lust shining in his brown eyes.

"Good boy."

I watched him go—because how could I not with a backside sculpted the way it was—closing my eyes only when he disappeared through the crowd. I willed a breath into my lungs, letting a good minute pass by before I headed in Aurelio's direction. Fae and humans of all shapes and sizes were in various states of undress—touching, kneading, taking, fucking. Their moans of pure pleasure echoed above the music drifting through the room. This level of debauchery was expected, encouraged even. This was the masquerade after all—sexual exploration and freedom were at the very essence of the festival. Everything sensual. Every desire met. To experience. To take.

To fuck.

The energy throughout the ballroom was palpable. It did nothing to ease the tension in my cock or the desire pumping through my veins. With slow, methodical steps, I ventured up the stairs to the rooftop oasis Aurelio and I had made our own over the decades of meeting in secret. When our pergola, resting under the starlit sky, came into view in the far corner, Aurelio's outline became visible. The sheer fabric that hung from the rafters did little to conceal the sight of him on his knees before the plush bed behind him. It robbed me of my breath.

Oh, the things I had planned for my little pet tonight.

I eased the curtain aside and approached my mate, who dutifully kept his gaze fixed on the floor at my feet. "You may look upon me," I instructed, as I slowly undid my cufflinks, my attention locked on him. I watched the hunger in his eyes grow with each button I unfastened on my dress shirt. "Are you ready for me, my pet?" I asked, throwing the shirt aside.

A grin threatened to emerge on his angelic face. "Yes, sir."

"Undo my trousers and take out my cock."

Aurelio bit that plump fucking lip, and it drove me positively wild. "Yes, sir."

As his fingers grazed my stomach, my dick jerked as he slipped the button free and undid the zipper, all the while keeping his hooded expression on me. And when my cock sprang forth, he licked his lips, and the urge to shove myself in his mouth became unbearable.

"Open your mouth."

His delectable mouth slowly dropped open on my command.

"Stick out your tongue. Yes, just like that. My, how marvelous you look, about to suck my cock. How ravenous you are for it. Now, wrap your hand around me." I hissed when the cool tips of his fingers slid around my hard length. "Mmmm. Yes, good boy. Give me a few good strokes. Ah, yes. Like that. Mmmm. Now, lick."

And lick, he did.

The tip of his tongue swirled around my raging head as Aurelio gathered every drop of precum upon it—his eyelids fluttering in this most enticing way.

"Goddess, you look so beautiful like this," I breathed. "On your knees for me. Ready. Willing. My needy little minx." My hands slid to the nape of his neck. "Now, suck."

Aurelio took it upon himself to pull my trousers down the rest of the way as he gripped my ass and pulled me all the way to the back of his throat. I couldn't help but gasp. And when he hummed, sending mind-blowing vibrations down my hardened shaft, my knees buckled slightly. The corner of his mouth curled into a wicked grin even as he took me deeper.

"Naughty, my pet."

My hips pulled away and immediately dove into his mouth anew. His gag shouldn't have been as erotic as it was, but, goddess, how sinfully erotic it was, how it fueled my need to dominate him. And as I began pumping in his warmth with abandon, I marveled at how he took me, how he was made for me.

Only me.

Drool slipped from the corner of his mouth. Like a naughty little cad determined to undo me, he gathered it on his fingers and guided it to my ass. My head tipped back as he pressed the slick finger into my opening. "Fuck." He was pumping in time to the thrust of my hips, driving me absolutely wild, working me like an instrument crafted for his desire. But, no. That wouldn't do. Tonight was about bringing him to his pleasure.

I pulled out of his mouth. "Up. I want you on the bed on your back. Now."

With feline grace and an expression of sin, Aurelio rose from the ground and slid onto the plush bedding behind him. I came around the bed, my focus solely on this male who drove my wildest inhibitions into a craze.

"Arms up."

As he obeyed my command with a look that bordered on adoration, my cock gave a painful throb. I took his wrist in my grip and reached for the leather cuff that lay hidden behind a pillow. Aurelio's eyes widened in surprise and... lust, perhaps?

"Oh, yes, darling. Those naughty fingers were interfering with my mission," I told him as I fastened his cuff and climbed onto the bed to straddle him. I reached for the matching cuff hidden on the other side, casting him a scandalous grin.

"And what mission is that?" he asked huskily, watching with hooded amber eyes as I fastened the other cuff.

At his question, I leaned toward him, breathing in the same air he exhaled in tiny, needy puffs. "To have you begging for my cock. I want your moans reaching the furthest corners of Atlantis." He whimpered when I rubbed my length against his in a slow roll of my hips. "I want them to hear your screams of pleasure all the way in the other realms." I lifted and reached for the pleasure oil on the nightstand. "I want there to be no doubt in the world who you belong to." I poured a generous amount into my palm, glaring at him with heated intensity all the while. His breath hitched as I raised his hips with one hand and smeared the substance through his crack, paying special attention to the puckered hole I planned to devour. "And I want everyone in the Starlit Masquerade to know it."

Without another word, I lined myself up to his tight channel and groaned as I slid my way home—the heat of him spurring me into an uncontrollable frenzy.

I fucked my mate.

Hard.

"Myles!"

Skin slapped against skin as I swiveled my hips in and out of his glorious ass. "Yes, my pet. Scream for me."

"Y-yes! Oh, my goddess! This feels too good," he called into the night. My fingertips dug into his hips as I plunged into him over and over and over again. Aurelio was a god brought to life, beauty personified, writhing beneath me as pleasure consumed every fiber of his being. And I was his master, relishing in every moment of it. "Fuck. I'm—"

I instantly pulled out of him, and his protest was cut short as I bent down and took his full, throbbing erection in my mouth. His gasp of surprise spurred me on. I sucked him with determination, letting the flat side of my tongue glide along his length. Gripping his base, I hummed with need as I bobbed my mouth on his cock.

"Oh fuck. Fuck!"

His seed spilled onto my tongue, and I drank it greedily, making sure to lap up all of his desire. But the need to be inside my mate had me rising to kneel between his legs, and flip him on his stomach. "On your knees."

Aurelio panted with exhaustion as he did exactly as I commanded—his tight, rosy hole displayed for my viewing pleasure. With a grunt, I entered my mate, and when he cried out, I massaged the muscles of his back. "You're doing so well, darling. Hang on." Thrust after thrust, I claimed him, molded to him. Never in a million years had I imagined a feeling like this. Our bond hummed between us, evidence of our destiny to be together—to shed the masks we wore if only for each other. My sacs began tightening as the telltale tingling sensation bloomed in my lower back, and I couldn't hold out any longer. "Relio!" He pushed his ass back, meeting my final thrust. I tipped my head to the stars as I came with the fury of a raging inferno. Nothing would ever come close to the feeling of making love to my mate.

Nothing.

After making quick work of his cuffs, I fell into the heap of pillows by his side and gathered his body into mine—his chest rising and falling against my pecs. And as our tongues twisted in a slow, sensual dance, I smiled into Aurelio's kiss, knowing we'd never part again. He was mine...

Forever.

THE END

Continue reading for a sneak peek of The Veiled Heir (The Heir of Atlantis, Book #1)

THE VEILED HEIR

SNEAK PEEK

Trying to calm my mind in the brutal Florida heat was like trying to read a book with someone banging on a drum next to my head. I tipped my head back, my lids closing against the sun's rays that scorched my tanned skin as I bobbed on the water—my abdomen tightening with the effort to keep steady. The warm summer breeze crested across the waters of the Atlantic, whipping my long, black hair behind my shoulders. Gentle waves pressed against my board as the palm trees hissed with the winds of change that had inevitably arrived, change that was now neatly packed into twenty-three boxes, one suitcase, and a toiletry bag that would be ready by morning.

The high-pitched squeal of children's laughter interrupted my moment of zen, and my eyes snapped open—my gaze landing on the group of people snorkeling a few paces away.

Not just any people.

Tourists.

Lots of them.

While they'd mostly followed the instructions I'd bellowed over the deafening roar of the boat's engine, it was clear most of them hadn't paid attention. Water periodically shot from their snorkel tubes like whales breaching the ocean's surface. It was difficult for them to keep their heads down long enough to catch the various fish species that populated the John Pennekamp Coral Reef State Park in Key Largo. No matter. I won't have to bellow any more instructions after today.

I reached down to cup the warm water and splashed it over my arms to cool my skin. Just thirteen more minutes, according to my Garmin; probably eleven since I'd checked about two minutes ago. The back of my neck prickled with awareness, prompting me to swivel around—my gaze catching on John Adams, the captain of our snorkel excursion tour boat. Deeply tinted aviator glasses rested upon the arrogant blade of his nose. His dark brown close-cropped hair remained flawless, and dark stubble shadowed his shapely jaw. The chiseled lines of his alluring mouth—one that had me desperate to move out of the friend zone this summer—formed a grin.

"Asshole," I murmured.

I could see John's shoulders shake with laughter even from this distance—quite the mouth reader, that one.

Watch the tourists, he said. It will be fun, he said. I resisted the urge to roll my eyes. The only reason John insisted I be the one who monitored our well-meaning customers was because I was a freak of nature. At least that's what I'd always called myself. My co-workers called me their good luck charm. The social media followers across Snorkida Shore Excursions' pages called me a viral sensation.

I'd rather do my job and be none of those things.

With my feet dangling in the water, I watched the man from Wisconsin barrel around again, attempting to right himself. Wisconsin's son popped his head out of the water and waved his hands in the air. "Chriiiiiiiiiiiiiis! I found one! I found one! Come quick!" he yelled.

In all her long-legged swimmer glory, Chrissy leapt from the boat's stern and gracefully swam the distance with minimal effort. Her Snorkida one-piece clung to her torso like a second skin as her body disappeared momentarily below. Despite the snorkel gear in hand, her muscular arms peeled through the water with natural strokes. The four years on the University of Miami swim team were precisely why I'd recommended her in the first place. While Chrissy Baker didn't have a marine biologist bone in her body, her bubbly personality played right into the hands of Snorkida's customers.

"What did you find, Sam?"

"The brightly colored one," he replied with an adolescent croak in his voice, his arms working feverishly to hold his body afloat.

Chrissy laughed. "They're all brightly colored, silly."

I could see the color bloom on the young man's pale cheeks from where I floated. "Right. Well. Um. The blue and yellow one."

"Ah, you're talking about a Blue Tang. The one with the yellow stripe?"

Sam pointed at her. "Yup, that's the one."

She put on one of her signature Chrissy smiles that had the hearts of men, both young and old, desperate to know her. "Then let's see if we can find it again, shall we?"

Damn, she really knows how to work 'em. That's another five-star review on TripAdvisor.

Chrissy fastened the snorkel gear skillfully over her ash-blond hair and dipped below water, searching for the fish she'd challenged the customers to find. She was notorious for claiming these fish were rare, but they were everywhere in these waters. "It's an attempt to make their experience special," she'd say, and judging by the number of people joining our excursion on any given day, I had no doubt that it was indeed working.

"Ash!"

I twisted around to John. A crease dipped below the top of his aviators as he pointed behind me. I wheeled back around, blocking out the sun with a raised hand. A hint of a fin slowly cut through the water a couple of dozen yards away.

It was heading in the direction of the tourists.

Without a second thought, I paddled feverishly for the boundary of the snorkel area—my board gliding on top of the surface. The muscles at my shoulders and biceps burned with each stroke. I instantly regretted packing those last few boxes before my shift. I'd have packed tomorrow before breakfast with my parents, but my driving desire for preparedness won over.

As I reached the perimeter, I bolted upright, willing air into my lungs. The fin slowed, slinking lazily back and forth in front of me.

Come on. Prove them wrong. Come at me.

But the shark did no such thing.

It transversed back and forth within ten yards from where I perched, my toned legs dangling below the water's surface in a tempting invitation.

So, we're going to do this dance again, are we?

Just when I thought this stand-off would last well after my shift was over, water splashed across my face, causing me to flinch. The shark retreated like it was being chased. I let out a long sigh. "They always do that," I muttered to myself. I allowed one final scan of my surroundings before paddling back to the boat.

The final guest climbed the ladder that dipped into the water at the stern. As I grabbed a rung, Chrissy stood above me with her hands on her hips, smirking. "Way to save the day, Aqua-woman."

I huffed a laugh as I climbed. "How fitting."

"You've certainly earned your happy hour slash celebratory farewell beer." Chrissy pulled me over the final rung of the ladder, and we began gathering the fins, goggles, and vests that littered the floor. My mind raced—as always—desperately trying to make sense of what happened as the engine roared to life.

Perhaps the little sharky was just used to humans?

It was a lie I greatly wanted my pulsing heart to believe.

With the equipment safely tucked away and Chrissy off to entertain the guests, I stomped up the stairwell to the top deck and slid into my usual seat beside John—his rough hands held firmly on the wheel. He spared a glance at me, and the corner of his mouth twisted into a smirk.

"Don't say it."

"I haven't said anything," John said with mock innocence dripping in his tone. When he bit his lower lip, I swatted his upper arm. He broke out in hysterical laughter that drifted over the sound of the engine. "I'm sorry. I'm sorry. It's just so weird."

I shook my head. "Don't remind me."

"But really cool at the same time, Ash." He gazed blankly into the distance, as if replaying the incident in his mind. "Every. Single. Time."

I shifted in my seat. I should have felt flattered by the awe in his voice, but confusion harbored that space. All my life, the most dangerous ocean predators seemed to avoid me. An unspeakable kinship had become the motivation to major in marine biology. Perhaps it was a kinship I'd been imagining, but as a semi-pro surfer, I'd witnessed firsthand the behavior of sea creatures when I was in their presence. I'd never revealed my obsession to anyone, but the 'why' of it all held my fascination in a death grip. Testing my limits always gave me an adrenaline rush. And I'd become addicted to it.

An old college memory came to mind.

My classmates and I had been invited to participate in a dive. There had been no shortage of sharks in the water that day, which was perfect for what I'd been eager to test. I recalled my classmate's ashen face and could still hear her screaming in the water around her mouthpiece.

I tested the limits with a raw piece of meat that I had stealthily brought into the water. I can still see the crimson blood drifting into the water from the bait that was gripped tightly in my hand. I remembered the great white shark that had emerged from the shadows. It had circled me a few times, making no move to eat the meat...or my arm. And I could still feel my heart nearly coming out of my chest. After a several-minute standoff between us, I abandoned the meat and swam for the surface, but not before I witnessed the shark return to devour the bait I'd left behind. After that, most of my classmates thought I was some sort of shark whisperer.

To myself, I would always be Asherah Rey Delmar, a freak of nature. To my classmates, surf pros, and co-workers, I'd been nicknamed the queen of the sea creatures. And I'd made it my life's mission to find out why.

Ready to dive in?

Click here to download your copy of The Veiled Heir (eBook readers) or scan below to purchase your copy of The Veiled Heir:

Acknowledgements

This book would not be possible without the inspiring love my LGBTQ+ friends and family have shown. Thank you for constantly demonstrating what it means to be part of a community where everyone feels loved, appreciated, and accepted—even a little fruit fly with big dreams of becoming an author. I will continue to advocate for you until my very last breath.

Brittany and Megan, thank you, as always, for all your contributions to my work. I appreciate you more than you'll ever know. Also, look at me not accidentally using an Acknowledgements template! There's hope for me yet! lol

Karisma, thank you so much for your constant efforts and patience. You've eased my anxiety two-fold. I appreciate you keeping me in line.

Mariah, Emeline, Graciela, Sarah, and Carliann, thank you so much for participating in the Starlit Desires collab. We made it!

And as always, to my amazing hubby, Brian, whose support is my north star in my authorship. I love you forever.

ABOUT THE AUTHOR

S.T. Fernandez (a.k.a. Stephanie) an award-winning author originally from Orlando, Florida. She now lives in the charming beach town of Ventura, California, with her husband and their two spirited wiener dogs.

Stephanie holds a Bachelor's degree in English Literature from Saint Leo University and has been a lifelong fan of romantic fiction, particularly fantasy and paranormal romance. As a proud BookFest Award winner, she crafts immersive stories that transport readers to vivid, emotional worlds filled with magic, passion, and heart.

When she's not writing or marketing like a mad woman, you'll likely find her on the patio soaking up the California sun, a glass of red wine in one hand and a book in the other—probably one with a swoon-worthy shadow daddy and a strong, unforgettable heroine.

Instagram: @stfernandezwrites | TikTok: @stfernandezwrites |
X: @stfernandez
www.stfernandez.com

www.ingramcontent.com/pod-product-compliance
Lightning Source LLC
Chambersburg PA
CBHW020041310726
48970CB00007B/2364